Home. **That annoying word again. A fantasy she had spent most of her life without.**

"Please, just make yourself at home," Leo offered politely.

Wondering if her thoughts had shown on her face, she snapped, "But it's not my home. Not anymore."

A gigantic lie, considering the contentment flowing into her soul since returning.

If she'd slapped him across the face, Gila doubted the impact would have been as robust. The shutters in Leo's eyes returned and closed her out. Those same much-hated shutters she'd seen so often during those last weeks before she left.

"I need to go out," Leo said, stepping away. "I'll see you tonight, unless you're already in bed."

"I will be," she said, her eyes drifting again to the bed. The one they'd shared for over a year. Where they'd laughed and made love. Where they'd confessed secrets and shared Sunday-morning tea mixed with buttered toast and laughter. The place where she'd believed they were their true selves. Where she'd sworn their love grew stronger.

And once again, the overpowering sense of returning home caused another break in her already-battered heart.

Dear Reader,

Sometimes people in relationships can behave in ways that end up emotionally hurting their partner. We all know how that feels, don't we? And that's exactly what's happened in *The Midwife's Nine-Month Miracle*. After Leo messes up big-time, Gila has to decide if she can ever forgive him and whether their marriage is worth saving. Add in the fact that she's also expecting their first child…and it's not an easy decision for her to make.

I loved writing Gila and Leo's story and I hope you enjoy getting to know them. If you do, please let me know. You can find me via my Twitter account, @sriversauthor, or pop over and say hello on Goodreads. I look forward to hearing from you.

Best wishes,

Shelley Xxx

THE MIDWIFE'S NINE-MONTH MIRACLE

SHELLEY RIVERS

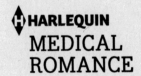

HARLEQUIN®
MEDICAL
ROMANCE™

Recycling programs
for this product may
not exist in your area.

ISBN-13: 978-1-335-73731-1

The Midwife's Nine-Month Miracle

Copyright © 2022 by Shelley Rivers

Harlequin Enterprises ULC
22 Adelaide St. West, 41st Floor
Toronto, Ontario M5H 4E3, Canada
www.Harlequin.com

Printed in U.S.A.

Shelley Rivers is a Bournemouth girl who spent most of her childhood reading. Married with a family, she now splits most of her time between reading, writing and pampering to the whims of her hilarious greyhound. Her hobbies include lopsided sewing, holey knitting and collecting old stuff that no one else sees the beauty in.

Books by Shelley Rivers

Harlequin Medical Romance

Tempted by the Brooding Vet
Awakening His Shy Vet
Reunited by Her Twin Revelation

Visit the Author Profile page at Harlequin.com.

To Don, whom the family lost during the writing of this book. I hope the dog walks in heaven are as good as the ones down here on earth.

And to Jean, one of the silent army of carers who are often forgotten. You did good, girl.

CHAPTER ONE

Mart's Medical Clinic, London

GILA WRIGHT RUBBED a hand over her stomach and tried not to laugh at the appalled faces being made by the seven teenage girls viewing the film depicting a birth scene. But every time she gave this class, the horrified expressions on the faces of the young mums-to-be as the reality of impending labour hit home always made her chuckle.

'It's a bit grim, isn't it?' one expectant mother commented with a deep frown, her fingers flipping the braided strap of her purple handbag.

'Don't worry,' Gila soothed with practised ease. 'You'll be too busy pushing your child out into the world to be concerned with anything else. It's all perfectly natural and survivable.'

None of the girls appeared overly convinced

by Gila's reassuring words. Each eager to do everything correctly during their pregnancy, while secretly dreading the actual event of impending childbirth and new motherhood. Gila understood their concerns. In less than a month, she too would be going through the whole process for the first time. Though at thirty-two years old she was far from being an unmarried teenager.

Since Mart's had opened two years previous, the walk-in clinic had run antenatal classes especially for teenage mothers. It had begun as a pilot scheme to help relieve the strain and workload on several of the area's local health practices. A place where young women could find help and information no matter what their circumstances were. Somewhere welcoming where the teenagers received no judgement or criticism. Just help, information and caring medical advice. The classes had proved so successful that a decision had been made to run them permanently, having become an important service to the neighbouring community, and many of the medical staff who worked at Mart's were actually volunteers who lived in the area and fitted in shifts around their main hospital jobs.

Gila had joined the staff two months ago,

after taking maternity leave from her position as a midwife at the local maternity unit. She spent two days a week volunteering at the clinic, rather than sitting around on her uncle's narrowboat, lonely and bored, with too much time to dwell on things she'd prefer not to.

Rubbing her hand lovingly over her baby bump again, she sent a silent prayer of thanks as the film ended, signalling the end of the week's session. Her back ached, her slightly swollen feet pinched against the insides of her flat black shoes, and she yearned to head home. And for the last hour she'd also craved sliced apples and thick toffee sauce with ridiculous intensity. Both of which she envisaged eating while lying in a warm relaxing bath.

'So, any questions?' she asked, returning her full attention to the circle of young women. 'This is our last group together before I leave to have *my* baby, so if you do think of anything before your next class with my colleague Sarah, who's taking over from me, remember you can speak to your individual midwives or family doctors. They are there to help. Nothing that is worrying you is silly or unimportant. I promise medics and midwives have heard everything before, no matter how crazy-sounding, so don't let embarrassment stop you. Okay?'

'I have a question,' asked a teenager, sticking up her hand as though still at school. 'How long before we let our partners back? You know, physically. Because after watching that—' she pointed at the now blank screen '—I'm thinking seriously about asking to be sterilised after the birth.'

Gila laughed and quickly mollified her. 'Depending on the birth, but usually we advise six weeks before resuming making love. I promise you'll soon forget about the messy side of giving birth the minute your baby settles in your arms. And if you want, I can suggest to Sarah that she talks about birth control options for after your babies arrive, at the next session.'

Several young mothers murmured their enthusiasm for the idea, before they all stood and shuffled towards the door, chatting and laughing as they filed out of the room. Each airing their opinion of what they had just watched.

Gila slowly rose from her chair, as a too familiar heavy silence and melancholy moved through her as the last young woman waved goodbye and closed the door. The difference between her and those seven young girls was that Gila knew for a fact that they would each be sharing the births of their first child with a partner at their side. Whether a boyfriend, mother or even a brother, each one fortunate to have someone with them cheering them on through the long hours of labour. Whereas Gila would face the birth of her child alone. The father of her baby would not be reassuring her with encouragement and loving words. Or holding her hand and whispering praise as the labour intensified. No, her child's father would be absent, just as he had been for the last four months of her pregnancy. Ever since the night she packed a bag and walked out on him.

She sighed and reached for the blue medical bag sitting in the centre of the large desk in the corner of the room. Afternoon sunlight cast its warmth into the area through the large window that faced out onto the clinic's car park, illuminating the normally invisible dust particles floating in the air. She empathised with those twisting and turning specks. Existing, yet not really having somewhere special to land and make a long-term home. A particular spot where they were really wanted.

Shoving several folders into the bag, Gila searched for the rest of her belongings. She was due to finish working at the clinic the following week, but each day she gathered a few more of her bits and pieces to take home rather than leave everything to the last day. She'd enjoyed volunteering at the clinic, but as her pregnancy advanced she found her energy sapping quicker with each passing week, often returning home utterly exhausted. She still had so much to organise before the baby came. Things she'd purposely put off, unwilling to do them alone. Hoping the situation with her baby's father might change and improve. But it hadn't, so it appeared that alone was exactly how she would be doing everything from now on. At least until the little one arrived.

She picked up her diary from the desk, her eyes falling onto the slim white band of skin on her left third finger. The place where her wedding ring once encircled. She'd removed it a week ago during a bout of tears and self-pity. One long lonely night, when the sight of it and everything it once represented mocked her one time too often for ever believing in happiness and love.

Her disruptive and unconventional childhood should have taught her better than to imagine that a normal happy life could finally be hers. That the pipe dream of a perfect marriage was actually achievable. Surely her own father's many destructive short-term relationships and incessant itch to wander the world, pursuing one false dream after another, should have taught Gila that simple truth didn't exist?

Yet despite knowing better, she'd hoped her relationship with her husband would be different. That it would last for ever and show everyone around them that she wasn't an undependable relationship car crash like her father, but a responsible adult who lived an ordinary, contented life. After all, she'd witnessed her parent's slip-ups so often, there was no chance she'd commit similar ones, was there?

Only, despite everything she'd thought and believed, it seemed she stupidly had.

In spite of all the promises she'd whispered to herself as a child on those nights when they'd slept on the pavements of unfamiliar streets because her father's money had run out and the hotel they'd been staying in had evicted them. Or the days when she would sit alone on a balcony while her father spent time with yet another woman he'd met and tumbled into mock love with. Left and ignored while they made love in another room. Gila had forgotten all of those promises and naively fallen in love with a man who turned out not to love her as deeply as she thought. And now she was weeks away from having their child and the solitude of the situation she found herself in seemed to increase with each and every passing day.

As she closed the bag, a knock on the door drew her attention from her sombre contemplations. Forcing a lightness she wasn't feeling into her tone and mood, she called out, 'Come in.'

Trudy, the afternoon receptionist, who dressed similar to a nineteen-fifties Hollywood starlet, opened the door and flashed Gila a cheerful smile. Tall and stylish, she reminded Gila of everything she was not.

'All finished for the day?' Trudy asked.

'Just packing up,' Gila replied with a smile she wasn't feeling. 'I'm glad it's nearly the weekend, though.' No longer working full-time at the hospital, she had the rare luxury of the whole Easter weekend free and she intended to enjoy every minute. Well, perhaps enjoy was too ambitious a goal, considering the wreck her private life was in, but she refused to spend further time wallowing. She intended to finish the lemon baby's blanket she'd started knitting a few weeks ago, despite the fact it looked nothing like the pattern's picture, and then make sure she'd bought everything she needed for the baby's imminent appearance.

'I've a ton of things to do,' she continued. Which wasn't quite true, but she doubted Trudy wanted to hear that her weekends were actually the worst part of the week because the days dragged like old arthritic toes through a puddle of treacle and gave her the unwanted opportunity to lull over how everything in her life had changed from being perfect and wonderful into a huge dreadful and horrible mess within the matter of months.

'I thought you'd want to know Reese Newman has walked in with her boyfriend, complaining of stomach pains. Any chance you can assist the doctor dealing with her? She behaves better with you.'

Reese, a teenager who was five months pregnant, struggled with every aspect of her pregnancy. She'd spent half of her life in foster homes and had been expelled from two schools, a fact she'd proudly informed Gila of the first time they met. She was also unfortunately rude and at times aggressive. She ignored most medical advice and spent her time following her on-off boyfriend as he committed one crime after another. She also had no settled home life or relationship with her birth parents, and loved nothing more than causing a scene.

Gila groaned softly and swung the bag onto her shoulder. Any other day she'd willingly deal with the girl's abrasive manner, but today she was just too exhausted. 'Must I?'

'She's with the new doctor right now,' Trudy said, leaning against the door frame. 'I doubt it's going well. You know what she's like with new people.'

'New doctor?' Gila asked, only half listening. Because a portion of the clinic's staff consisted of volunteers, it wasn't unusual for medics to come and go. Some stayed for a few months, others only a few days or weeks.

'Wait until you see him,' Trudy said with a grin. 'The man's gorgeous. Sexier than a top-ten heart-throb. Has lovely wavy dark hair that hits his shoulders.' She tapped her own and smiled dreamily. 'Makes a woman think all sorts of naughty thoughts about tugging it.'

'I thought Dr Peters worked on Friday afternoons,' Gila said, walking towards the door. Dr Peters headed the Accident and Emergency department at the local hospital, but volunteered several days a week at the clinic. She knew him well, but so far they'd both covered different shifts, so she hadn't seen him during the weeks she'd been working at the clinic.

'Normally he does, but he's had to rush off to America to be with his daughter. Something about her child's been taken ill and it's not looking good. So he's arranged for this new doctor to step in for a couple of weeks to cover his Tuesday, Wednesday and Friday shifts. I swear my knees shook when the man walked in and spoke to me. Gorgeous brown eyes. Like pools of melted truffles. Rich and completely bad for a female's peace of mind. And his deep voice—wow.'

'Really?' Gila asked, mostly because Trudy expected it than any real interest in the new doctor. She was off men for good and wasn't in the mood to drool over another handsome one. Besides, this advanced in her pregnancy the only salivating she did involved toffee-covered edibles. Doctors were especially off her menu.

'How about a cup of raspberry tea before you go?' Trudy suggested, moving back so Gila could step out of the room and into the corridor.

Gila winced at the idea, sickness creeping up her throat. She swallowed away the undesired taste and shook her head. She really wanted to go home, but, conscious of not wanting to be considered grumpy, she said, 'If you have ginger and lemon, I'll consider it. Raspberry tea just reminds me of morning sickness.'

Trudy laughed as they walked along the corridor and headed towards the consultation rooms. 'It's jam sandwiches for me. Someone told me during my pregnancy that they helped with alleviating morning sickness when I was carrying my twins, and to some degree they did, but now I can't stand the smell of strawberry jam without wanting to run for the nearest bathroom. So are you looking forward to becoming a mum?'

This time Gila's smile was genuine. 'I can't wait.'

'Do you know what you're having?'

'No, I want it to be a surprise,' she said, and in an effort to change the subject before it became even more personal, she asked, 'Which consultation room is Reese being seen in?'

Trudy pointed to the one at the far end of the corridor. 'Room three. Don't forget to pop into the staff room before you leave. No sneaking off home hoping I won't notice.'

Gila forced another smile, and promised, 'I won't.'

Moving in the direction of the consultation room, she rubbed a hand over her stomach once more. If Reese was in an awkward mood, Gila would need a ton of patience, because a sixth sense warned her that the next few minutes were going to be tough. She just didn't realise how right that prediction would actually turn out to be.

Leo Wright listened to the pregnant patient and frowned. Both she and the young man who'd accompanied her had continued to complain and bicker since stepping into the consultation room. Despite several attempts to intervene and discover the reason for their visit, Leo still had no idea what ailed the young woman. The only clue he'd gathered while observing her movements was the way she kept wincing and placing a hand to the right side of her stomach.

'Reese, perhaps if you'd just compose yourself,' Leo suggested, keeping his voice low, patient and friendly. 'Then we might be able to work out what it is that has brought you to the clinic today.'

'In other words, stop whingeing, and let the doctor help ya,' her boyfriend grumbled, his eyes not shifting from the screen of his phone.

Leo sighed when the young couple resumed arguing. The only reason he stood in this bland, unfamiliar room was because he owed his boss the biggest favour and he secretly wanted a chance to see his wife. Small glimpses from the window of his home were usually all he caught thanks to the fact that, despite leaving him and their home, she still resided close by. Brief moments where he mostly stared at her back as she walked away. For the last few weeks he'd suspected Gila of avoiding him. They needed to sort things out between them soon. The odd text and email concerning their unborn baby was not enough. This lack of real communication had continued for too long. Their baby's birth was mere weeks away and it was vital for him to be involved. He desperately wanted to be closer than he was right now. In what capacity he didn't care, but this silent stand-off and purposely skirting around each other wasn't helping either of them.

The time had come to try and fix the wrong he'd committed. He now understood that, without meaning to, he'd hurt the one precious person in his life. His wife. His Gila.

Every part of him wanted to beat and howl against the agony of knowing that he'd shattered her trust. That he alone had caused the anguish in her beautiful grey eyes and broken her world apart. He'd damaged their marriage and taken the most wonderful, tender woman and wrecked her. And why? Because the turmoil that had developed inside his heart after his sister's death had grown so big and powerful, he'd pushed everyone who mattered away. Not capable of dealing with the overwhelming guilt that had consumed him, he'd retreated into himself, when he should have clung to his wife, the way a dying man clutched to breath and hope.

Last November his kid sister, Jodie, died from a drugs overdose. One he'd failed to save her from. All the years of learning and practising medicine. Years poring over medical books and passing practical tests and for what? So he could help strangers, yet when his own sick sister had desperately required his help, he'd been useless to stop her addiction and keep her alive. Even worse, guilty of turning her away when she'd needed him the most.

For three days, Leo had sat by Jodie's hospital bedside, praying for her to wake up from a coma, but in the end she'd silently given up and slipped away. Leaving this world without giving him the chance to say sorry or goodbye.

And for weeks after, the sorrow and the misery had swamped everything in Leo's life. Catching him at quiet moments, the remorse had chewed at his conscience and gnawed at his heart.

Instead of seeking comfort in his wife's arms, Leo had turned from Gila, not wanting to drag her into the bleak levels of despair that ate at him. Reluctant to admit his part in Jodie's death to anyone. If Gila had learnt the truth, she would have stopped seeing him as a protector, and viewed him as nothing but a failure. He would cease to be the hero he suspected his wife secretly viewed him as, leaving him exposed as nothing but a useless man incapable of protecting and helping a loved one. An incompetent doctor unable to heal.

Then after weeks of his pretending that everything was fine, hiding the agony inside him, everything had finally tumbled down and smothered Leo completely, ridding him of sane thought and normal behaviour. He'd withdrawn into his internal hell of regret and blame until he'd become aware of nothing but the darkness and the shame.

Even now, months later, he didn't understand why he'd reacted in that way. Or why he'd hurt the one person he truly loved.

Closing his eyes, Leo silently repeated the words his grief counsellor suggested he say every time the past's emotions threatened to resurface. With his counsellor's help he'd started the journey through the self-reproach, depression and sorrow. It wasn't an easy or fast process, but with each weekly session he was slowly accepting Jodie's death and putting everything into its proper context. His behaviour and the decisions he'd made before his sister's passing hadn't cause Jodie's death. With his counsellor's help, he was beginning to see that.

A counsellor his boss, Dr Peters, had insisted he visit, after recognising the signs of anxiety and depression in Leo. Without his boss's help, Leo doubted he'd still have a career or his job at the local hospital's A & E. It was also Peters who'd come to him the previous day, in a terrible state, and begged him to temporarily take over his weekly shifts at Mart's, so that he could leave the country to be with his daughter and seriously sick grandchild. Without hesitation, Leo had agreed. Happy to do whatever favour the man asked, though how his estranged wife was going to react when she found out he would be working at the clinic, Leo didn't want to consider. But the chance to help and repay his boss as a work colleague and a friend took priority.

Returning his attention to the young woman sitting on the examination table, he suggested, 'How about you tell me why you're holding your hand to your side?'

Again she ignored him.

'Does it hurt there?' Leo coaxed.

'I ain't talking to you,' the teenager snapped.

A knock on the door prevented him from replying. With a curt nod at the female, he strolled over to the door and flung it open. And finally encountered the woman who haunted his every thought.

Gripping the handle, Leo lowered his gaze and took in the shape of their growing child beneath her too large, shapeless blue uniform. A child he desperately wanted to be close to. His flesh and blood, his contribution to his future family. Boy or girl, he didn't care. He just wanted to be its father. Somehow, he had to repair his relationship with Gila enough to be able to do that. He just hoped for their unborn child's sake it wasn't an impossible mission.

'Hello, Gila,' he said softly. 'Won't you come in?'

'Leo?' Gila's heart stopped as her brain tried to make sense and acknowledge the man standing in the doorway. For the last few months she'd avoided him, other than the odd text to keep him up to date on the baby's health and development, but here he was in the one place she'd considered herself safe from his presence.

Gripping the canvas straps of her bag, she forced her legs to keep her upright and not collapse into a crumpled heap the way the rest of her body suddenly longed to. How would Leo react if she did? Would he care enough to scoop her up from the floor, or would he leave her where she landed in a pool of shock and body parts and ignore her as he'd done for the last few months? Just pretend she didn't exist and was no concern of his.

She didn't trust in coincidences. She did however believe in bad luck, and it appeared that life had again chosen to dump another reeking bucketful slap bang in her path.

'Finally,' a female voice complained behind Leo. 'Someone I know. Here, Miss Wright, will you tell this man to leave me alone?'

'Sorry,' Gila stammered, her heartbeat thundering like a thousand drumming fingers. 'I must have the wrong room.'

Trembling, she half turned, desperate to get away from the man and the swoosh of memories initiated from one glance of his handsome face. Strong features whose hard plains she'd once traced and scattered with kisses and reverence. Bronze skin, sometimes smooth, occasionally covered with dark bristles that tickled her fingertips and prickled her own flesh in places only he had ever uncovered and explored.

'Gila.'

She stiffened at the sound of her name falling from his lips after so many weeks of silence and glanced back. The bright artificial light in the corridor giving her a view of the man she'd once adored, before he'd destroyed all that they'd shared.

She shook her head and moved away. Not even for Reese and her baby's well-being could Gila walk into the room and pretend that the man she'd once loved wasn't there with them. That he didn't stand less than a foot away. That his familiar body didn't dominate the space, reminding her of things she'd spent weeks and days deliberately closing her mind from. No, she couldn't do it. Not even for a patient. For once, not this time.

For long torturous weeks, she'd worked to regather the fragments of her shattered life. With no other choice, she'd forced the pain of Leo's abandonment to one side, refusing to face it, instead throwing herself into her work. And now, when she'd finally believed she had found a balance, here he appeared to upend and unsettle her calmness once again.

'No. I'm sorry, I must—'

'Gila, wait.'

The deep words wrapped around her, tempting and provoking. Wasn't it enough that Leo tortured her dreams, causing her to continually replay their last conversation when he'd proven that everything she'd imagined true about their relationship was nothing but a lie?

'No,' she whispered again, lowering her eyes. She couldn't do this. It was too late, or maybe too soon for this encounter.

He reached for her, but she jerked away, not wanting his touch. Once she'd craved his fingers on her body, desired the firm stroke of his caress upon her skin, now the thought made her stomach ache and her skin prickle.

This man once slipped a gold ring onto her finger in front of a church full of family and friends. A church not three miles from here. Then he'd professed to worship and love her for six wonderful months of perfect marriage, before discarding her from his life like an unwanted curio he'd simply grown bored of playing with.

'Oi, Miss Wright,' Reese called, oblivious to the tension between the two professionals. 'I want to speak to you.'

Leo stepped back and refocused on the patient. 'Miss Newman, you came here because you said you required help. Other patients wait in Reception. Ones who truly want our assistance. So unless you wish to sit for hours in the nearest hospital's A & E, I suggest you tell me exactly what is wrong.'

Pushing all emotions and private desires aside, Gila swallowed her reluctance and pride and stepped into the room. Moving over to where Reese waited, she took control of both the situation and the argumentative teenager. 'Reese, tell Dr Wright, what's the problem? He can help you.'

Reese pouted and folded her arms.

Gila sighed softly and used her best no-nonsense midwife voice. Knowing this was the best way to deal with the girl. Not taken in by the tough front Reese frequently hid behind when scared. She recognised the insecurity and self-doubt in the young woman as the same form that once sat in her own uncertain heart. Convinced that the world viewed you with disdain and disgust, simply because your home life differed from the standard model. What she'd learnt through her work as a midwife was that there was no standard family. Every single one was different.

'Because you're here for a reason,' she continued. 'And I'm sure it isn't to waste our time. So, are you in pain? You're very pale. Are you taking the iron tablets I prescribed for you?'

Reese shrugged guiltily. 'I lost them.'

'I'll write you a new prescription before you leave. It's important that you take them. So, where's the pain?'

Reese sighed, then, with a resentful glare at her boyfriend, stated, 'I'm not being a baby. Everyone thinks I am, but it really hurts here in my side. I vomited several times, too. I thought it was just the pregnancy, but I don't know. Something don't feel right.'

Leo moved closer but continued to let Gila lead the consultation.

'Reese, will you allow me to check you over while Dr Wright observes?' Gila asked.

'Go ahead.' Reese sighed, amazingly complacent now someone was listening to her fears. She glanced worriedly at Gila, vulnerability shining from her young, troubled eyes. 'Do you think there's something wrong with the baby?'

'Let's not worry yet,' Gila soothed, patting her arm. 'Now lie down and can you tell me exactly where the pain is and how it feels? Is it a dull pain? Or perhaps a stabbing kind of pain?'

She gently placed her fingers to the teenager's stomach on the right side, below her baby bump. 'If I press here, does it hurt more when I pull my fingers away or less?'

Reese gasped as Gila drew her fingers away. With a glare, she answered, 'More.'

Gila glanced at Leo, seeing the same suspicion in his eyes. 'And you say you've suffered bouts of sickness?'

'Yes.' Reese nodded.

Leo smiled reassuringly and glanced at Gila. 'Okay, well, I suspect it's a grumbling appendix. What do you think?'

'Highly likely,' Gila agreed with the prognosis, having come to the same conclusion.

Leo took over now they'd both agreed on the possible cause of Reese's pain and discomfort. 'I'm going to call for an ambulance to drive you over to the main hospital and once you're there the doctors can run tests and find out exactly what is going on.'

'Is it dangerous?' asked Reese's boyfriend. 'She ain't going to lose the kid, is she?'

Leo faced the man. 'I'm not going to lie to you. In severe cases it can be life-threatening. It's important Reese goes to the hospital and gets it checked out. This isn't an issue you should ignore or leave.'

Gila helped Reese down from the examination table. 'I'll write out a new prescription for the iron tablets and meet you in Reception. Do not leave before I give it to you. Okay?'

Gila followed the young couple out of the room, ignoring Leo, who stood watching her. She'd done her job and helped with Reese, but that was all she owed the man who didn't care that he'd broken her heart. Or that he'd taken all her stupid secret precious daydreams and shattered every single one.

CHAPTER TWO

'Surprise!'

Gila jumped and stared at the small group of colleagues crammed into the tiny staff room, and almost gave into the urge to run for the closest exit. She wanted to flee from the building, or in her case waddle quickly away from all the people now grinning expectantly at her.

Doctors, nurses, receptionists, even the clinic's office staff gawked back at her with bright eager faces waiting for a reaction. She immediately regretted not leaving after seeing Reese into the ambulance, but her conscience had battled against the impulse and she'd reluctantly headed to the staff room intending to drink a cup of fruit tea with Trudy and leave as quickly as possible.

But that resolution wasn't going to be doable now because it was clear that any chance to escape for home was a long way off.

So this was the real reason why Trudy had insisted she join her for refreshments, despite it being the end of Gila's shift. The other woman obviously planned to inflict social hell, wrapped up in a thoughtful act, on her. Gila's gaze flickered to the brightly wrapped pile of gifts in Trudy's hands. Oh, great, another baby shower. She'd already endured this public agony with her other colleagues at the hospital before starting her official maternity leave. When she'd had to pretend that everything was hunky-dory in her life, and not show any hint that their act of kindness made her want to buckle into a pile of uncontrollable sobs. And now her colleagues at the clinic, with this touching and sweet deed, left her feeling the same way. Only this time, thanks to her recent run-in with Leo, she feared she didn't have the strength to hide her inner heartache.

Forcing back tears, she forced her mouth into a wobbly smile and hoped her acting skills weren't too horrendous or lacking. 'I don't know what to say.'

'It's just a few small things for the baby,' Trudy quickly explained as she crossed the room and gently drew Gila inside. The firmness of the woman's grip on her arm hinted that Gila's acting skills must really suck. 'We wanted the baby to have something special, so we all clubbed together and purchased these few gifts for you to remember us by.'

Touched, Gila sensed movement behind her and almost let the tears fall when she turned her head to find Leo staring at her. Standing in the doorway, his white doctor's coat now replaced by a familiar black jacket and faded blue jeans. Part of her yearned to rush across the room and bury herself in his arms.

Trudy was spot on when she described Leo as gorgeous. Handsome in a rough, square-jawed kind of way. Brown kind eyes, thick wavy brown hair that curled on his shoulders. His nose slightly crooked, thanks to a moped accident as a teenager. In truth, his features should have created a face full of imperfections, yet the opposite was true. They sat together in perfect accord. As though the clever fingers of a super-talented sculptor had carefully and lovingly carved them over long hours and many days. Not stopping until the features were perfect.

Gila turned away and allowed Trudy to hand over the presents and lead her towards the others. She dragged up her fake and much used, though utterly despised, happy face. The one she'd formed as a second skin over the last few months. The expression she only dropped when alone, so no one would guess her true internal misery.

Stammering, she said to the group, 'Y-you shouldn't have gone to all this trouble.'

Though her attention appeared to be on the others, her mind crammed and twisted with questions concerning the man standing behind her. Even with space between them, she could feel his presence as though he were imprinted on her flesh like a permanent mark. What was Leo doing here at the clinic? Trudy had mentioned Dr Peters had asked him to take over, but Leo wasn't some junior doctor, eager to do his boss's bidding to win favour or promotion. He'd worked his way to the position of Dr Peters's second in command and he loved his job in A & E. So why come to the clinic? It didn't make any sense. Surely someone else could have taken the man's place.

She again caught sight of the man troubling her thoughts. He'd moved further into the room and now held a very large, ultra-adorable cuddly toy giraffe half tucked underneath his arm. Its sweet furry face stared back at her.

Everything was wrong with this scenario. Fresh tears threatened to overflow as she regarded the man she'd until recently loved. She yearned to leave this room full of happy, cheerful people and crawl into some private, hidden hole, because the man who'd helped create their baby now stood holding a toy giraffe looking as uncomfortable as she was, but also meltingly gorgeous. No one at the clinic knew who her husband was, and she didn't intend to admit the new doctor standing paces away was the father of her unborn child, or that their marriage sat in tatters. Right now all she wanted to do was get through the next ten minutes without having an emotional meltdown.

How would she survive working at the clinic and seeing Leo? Maybe she should leave today and let the clinic find another midwife to take over her last two days. Use the frequent bouts of tiredness that constantly dogged her as an excuse to finish a week earlier than planned. This clinic for the last few months had become her sanctuary, away from her worries and concerns. Where she dealt with other people's problems and health concerns. Each patient an ideal distraction from the mess of her own life.

And Leo wasn't just any man or doctor. He was so much more than that. He'd once been her everything. Her life. Her dreams. Her all.

Biting her lower lip to stop herself from bursting into tears, Gila pulled her gaze from

Leo. She knew more than anyone that crying was a waste of time. Did tears bring relief and peace? No, all they achieved was to lower her mood and leave her miserable.

Leo and Trudy rejoined them. Handing Gila several cards, Trudy explained, 'Dr Peters bought and sent over the giraffe that Leo is modelling so well.'

Gila smiled and for the first time in weeks a small wave of pleasure ran through her. She'd met Dr Peters many times through Leo and his work. Goodness knew what the man thought of her now. Did he consider her a dreadful woman for walking out on her husband so soon after the loss of his sister? People tended to take sides when a couple parted. Had he taken Leo's? But if so, why buy the giraffe?

'How kind of him,' she said, turning to the cuddly toy. Careful to avoid making eye contact with Leo, she slid a hand over it, gasping softly when her fingertips unexpectedly brushed his own hidden beneath the plush fur.

'Sorry,' she whispered, conscience of the wave of spiralling heat travelling up her arm from the contact. Snatching her hand away, she turned her attention back to the others stood close.

'Leo,' Trudy gushed, focusing her attention on the silent man. 'Why don't you rest the giraffe on a chair? Now your shift is over, I can introduce you to everyone. You've already met Gila, of course.'

Gila stayed silent as the couple moved away, dropping the huge giraffe onto a vacant plastic chair on their way. She didn't need to watch Leo making friends to know the concept of continuing to work here would be too hard to endure. Even for a few days. If one of her patients faced a similar situation, she'd recommend either they talked to their boss about a replacement for the newcomer, or that they consider leaving their job.

Somehow, she didn't think the clinic would accept her not wanting to work in the same building as her estranged husband as an acceptable excuse to ask Leo to leave. Not when Dr Peters obviously wanted him here. And as she was a volunteer midwife, on the verge of leaving, it made more sense that she'd be the one to go.

She sighed and glanced down at the pile of presents and cards. Why did Leo have to turn up a few days before she was due to leave? Had he done it on purpose?

Someone handed her a plastic cup filled with weak orange squash. Accepting it, she glanced casually at the clock on the wall. How long before she could leave without appearing rude? Would fifteen minutes be enough? Or should she stay longer?

'Don't worry,' Trudy said, joining Gila once again. 'Cluster of new patients just walked into Reception eager to keep this lot busy, so you'll be able to head off in a few minutes.'

Gila sighed and asked guiltily, 'Am I that obvious?'

'No, but you're eight months pregnant and I remember how that feels. I spent the last few weeks of my pregnancy switching from wanting to organise my entire house and taking naps whenever the chance arose.'

Gila smiled, liking the woman a little bit more. 'I'm ready for one right now, to be honest.'

Trudy laughed, then pointed across the room at the male conversing with two female staff members. 'Well, Leo's proving a hit. I sense he is going to be a great asset to the clinic.'

Which made Gila want to weep as the two women vied for her husband's attention. How would they react if she marched over there, grabbed Leo by the face and kissed him fully on the mouth? Or shouted across the room that he belonged to her and she wanted him back?

Which, of course, she didn't. Not any longer. But even so.

A silly hysterical giggle worked up her throat and she coughed to cover the sound before she embarrassed herself. The bleeping of her phone distracted her from the trio across the room. Retrieving it from her bag, she glanced at the screen and saw the alarm had gone off even though she couldn't recall setting it.

'I'm sorry, Trudy,' she lied. 'But I really must leave. I'm meeting someone.'

Trudy nodded and smiled. 'Let me ask Leo to carry the giraffe out for you.'

'No, really, I can manage,' she insisted, not keen to spend any more time around the man. She planned to enjoy her maternity leave and focus on nothing but the baby. Any decisions about Leo and the future could wait. She had some savings, and living rent-free on her uncle's narrowboat while he toured the wineries in France kept her expenses low and affordable.

'Nonsense,' Trudy dismissed. 'To be honest, I rather like seeing him carrying it. The giraffe suits him. I wonder if he has any children. Do you think he's married? Since my divorce I've been off men, but for him I'd dust off my sexy undies.'

'I doubt it,' Gila said, throwing him one last glare before gathering up the large toy with her free arm. 'He looks like the type of man who would be all words and empty promises.'

Trudy glanced back at her with a frown. 'Do you think so?'

Gila nodded. 'Only a fool would fall in love with a man like him. Trust me on that.'

'Gila.'

Gila's heartbeat skipped, but she ignored the man walking beside her along the long corridor that led to the clinic's front reception. Surely, he'd get the hint if she didn't speak to him? She'd made a point of keeping all contact between them centred only on their unborn child.

'Gila, please. I want to talk to you.'

'Sorry,' she stammered, her heartbeat thundering harder. Hugging the giraffe to her front, she said, 'I need to be somewhere. I don't have the time.'

It was all a lie, but she certainly didn't have the inclination to talk to him. Why didn't he just return to the staff room and resume his conversation with the other staff members? Go and bother them instead of her?

Trembling, she increased her speed, desperate to get away from the man and the swoosh of memories initiated from being around him. Memories of happy times when everything on the planet was wonderful and she believed she'd found a good man. Long before he ruined it all.

'Gila, please.'

Frustrated, she asked, 'What do you want, Leo?'

For weeks, she'd desperately worked to pick up the slivers of her splintered life and carry on. To put his rejection to one side and move forward. And now she refused to allow him to drag her backwards into the tempestuous well of emotions she'd spent so long battling to survive. Some days she'd wondered if she ever would. On others, why she even cared. So why now did Leo suddenly want to talk? Why not months ago when she'd knelt in front of him, clutching his hands while begging him to speak to her? When it might have mattered and made a difference?

'Please, Gila. Give me a chance to explain.'

The words enveloped her, tempting and teasing her with the past. Wasn't it enough that he still occupied her thoughts too much. 'No,' she whispered. She wasn't ready to do this. She didn't want to face anything, especially not here at the clinic. She refused to become the latest gossip amongst her colleagues.

Leo raised his hand as though to touch her, before dropping it again. Once she'd hungered and revelled in the firmness of his stroke, now she resented the idea.

Leo moved closer, his firm, square chin lifting in determination. 'It's time for us to talk, Gila. Really talk. Not by texts or emails the way we have been, but a proper face-to-face conversation. We need to reach some sort of understanding before the—'

She clasped the cuddly toy harder, her fingers crushing its plush softness. Trying hard not to breathe in the familiar woody aroma of Leo's aftershave as he invaded her area. An expensive brand she'd once saved all her spare money to buy him not long after they'd first met. 'Why your sudden need for a discussion, when for months you've ignored my existence?'

'That's not true,' he denied. 'I haven't ignored you. I've answered every text or question you've sent. I thought only to give you time and because my—'

Gila closed off his excuses, no longer interested. This man whom she'd handed her heart, together with her trust, didn't deserve her time. This man whose laughter and love-making once filled her body and spirit so completely had let her down. Badly. He'd done just as everyone else in her life had. Abandoned her when things became hard.

A deep frown creased Leo's forehead. 'This stand-off between us is helping no one.'

'Whose fault is that?' she hissed. She swallowed, her stomach rolling with fresh anger and resentment. Shaking her head, she closed the space between them and spat, 'How long are you going to be working here?'

Wasn't letting their marriage go enough of a crime to commit against her? Did he truly expect her to meekly work alongside him as though nothing linked them? As though he hadn't ripped her heart from her body and almost obliterated her?

'Let's go somewhere private and I'll explain everything,' he suggested. 'Once we talk—'

'How long?' she demanded again, refusing to move until she got an answer from him.

He sighed. 'I'm not sure. For the next few weeks at least. Dr Peters needs to be with his family.'

'Haven't you hurt me enough, Leo?' she asked. 'How dare you come to the clinic where I volunteer? Wasn't there someone else who could have stepped in? Didn't it occur to you that I wouldn't want you here? Is that why you didn't tell me? Well, I refuse to work in the same building as you.'

'I know it's not ideal, but I owed the man, Gila.' He stepped closer, dark brown eyes clashing with hers. 'Just let me explain.'

'No!' she snapped, her chest heaving as her legs wobbled. Stepping away, she bumped back into the edge of a table placed against the wall. A couple of leaflets stacked on top fell and floated to the floor.

Leo shook his head. 'Look, I'm sorry, Gila. For being here, for not thinking to tell you beforehand and for...well...everything.'

'I don't care,' she replied coldly. She didn't. Not any more. His apology meant nothing. Where was he during those first few days after she'd left? When she'd sat like an idiot in her uncle's narrowboat, constantly listening for the sound of his footsteps or his knock on the door? Convinced it would only be a short while before he came and begged her to go home. The anxious ritual of waiting for his appearance night after night, day after senseless day, now seemed ridiculous and infantile.

While she'd whispered a thousand prayers into the dark, silent hours, hopeful that they could mend what had torn them apart, he'd done nothing but shatter the few illusions she'd had left by staying away. Not once making contact during those first few days. Leaving her to wallow in pain and confusion.

Every emotion, all her devotion, every drop of her love for him had slipped away over those first few weeks apart. Running into the invisible drain of yet another broken relationship. Yet another let-down by someone who'd lied when they'd said they cared.

'I hate you,' she whispered. 'Don't you get that? What I once felt for you is gone. Now I simply hate you for proving what a fool I was to trust you.'

He flinched at her soft words, his expression turning emotionless and hard. 'I understand, but…'

She walked away, despite her unsteady legs still threatening to give way. She refused to crumble here in front of this man. This time there would be no crying or pleading the way she had before. This time she would walk away with her head held high, her future safe and protected deep inside her body.

Instinctively, she touched a free finger to her stomach, vaguely aware of the baby inside reacting with a gentle kick. Did her child sense that the man who had helped to create its life now reminded Gila of everything she'd lost? Of a love she no longer retained and suspected she never really had? That the true affection in their marriage had only come from her? And that fact hurt more than any of the disappointments from her past. The bitter, cruel knowledge that, yet again, neither she nor her love had really mattered.

Leo gazed after Gila as she rushed down the corridor. A piece of his heart slowly tearing at the speed she used to get away from him. Once they'd hurried to meet each other, now the woman raced away as though he risked her very existence.

She hated him. He'd expected it. Understood her anger, but the words she'd spat at him still pierced his soul. Seeping into the broken joints and cracks that continuously craved for her healing. A cure only she could instigate and perform. And something he now knew he would never obtain.

He should have called her when he'd found out yesterday that Dr Peters needed him to cover his shifts, but he hadn't thought—no, that wasn't true—he hadn't allowed himself to consider the complications his arrival here at the clinic might cause for his wife. Preferring to wait and deal with Gila's reaction in person instead of over the phone or through a text or email. In retrospect it had been cowardly and a mistake. Not warning her had just delivered another bad mark against himself when he already bore so many.

How could he make things right when she refused to listen? When she loathed being anywhere near him, and love no longer shone from her pretty grey eyes, which now held mistrust, dislike and pain.

He had caused the damage to their relationship and instead of rushing after her when she'd left, that night four months ago, he'd buried his head in his own agony and blocked out anyone else's wishes and needs. He'd acted like a selfish fool. A person he'd never believed he would ever become. Someone he didn't even understand or recognise.

He'd treated Gila as though she didn't matter, and that was what she couldn't forgive. He saw it in every movement and glance she sent his way. The hurt and disappointment of his being just another person who'd let her down after solemnly promising on their wedding day that he never would. Through her eyes, he saw her heart shouting out the unforgivable truth that he'd failed her.

Lowering his own gaze, he frowned at the small gift lying on the floor where, moments ago, Gila stood. Crouching, he picked it up, smiling at the cuteness of the bright yellow wrapping paper printed with orange rabbits. This gift had been bought for his child. Yet he'd stood in the staff room moments ago and watched everyone congratulate Gila without saying a word while the impulse to yell that he was the baby's father had almost crushed him. To let everyone in the room know that he was not some faceless stranger, but Gila's husband. The man who, in spite of his thoughtless actions, had never stopped loving her.

He clutched the gift and glanced in the direction that Gila had disappeared. She'd obviously dropped it in her rush to get away. To escape him and everything between them.

Straightening, he followed the same path. Determination in each stride. With luck he'd catch up with his wife before she left the car park. Whether she wanted it or not, they were going to talk face to face and not through some electrical means the way they had for the last few months. For the sake of his future relationship with his child, he'd fight for more.

Pushing open the clinic's glass entrance door, he paused to search the parked cars in front of him. Catching a glimpse of a familiar blue uniform, he headed after Gila, concerned when he spotted her resting against a black vehicle. He frowned as he took in the way she leaned over, one hand on the car's bonnet, head bent over as though having trouble breathing.

Quickly weaving through the remaining cars that separated them, he finally reached her side and demanded, 'Are you all right?'

Gila glanced up, her cheeks drained of all healthy colour. 'Leo?'

'What's wrong?' he asked, closing the gap between them. Something ailed his wife or their baby. Either way, he refused to leave them until he'd found out what.

'Nothing. I'm just feeling a little faint,' she answered. The words reluctant and dragged out as though she'd prefer to admit to anything else but the truth to him.

'How long?' he quizzed, reaching for her elbow.

'Just a few moments.'

'Why don't we go back inside the clinic and sit for a minute? Just until the feeling passes,' he suggested, relieved when she didn't pull out of his hold. Though the fact that she was letting him touch her at all increased his concern.

She shook her head. 'No, I want to go home, and my bus is due soon.'

'Forget the bus,' he dismissed, troubled by

this unexpected show of vulnerability from his wife. Gila's unsettled and unconventional childhood had taught her to guard her feelings with a hard outer shell. She rarely showed her softer side, unless she was truly comfortable with a person. 'There's always a later one or I can give you a lift home.'

She sniffed and shook her head again. 'No, thanks. I'd rather walk.'

'Don't be silly, Gila,' he scolded gently. 'It's not as if we're not going in the same direction, is it? Besides, aren't you meeting someone?'

She ignored his question and replied, 'It makes no difference. I'll get the bus.'

'Gila...'

'Don't,' she warned. 'I just want to go home.'

'Okay,' he said, noticing how weary she looked. 'You clearly want no part of me and I understand that.'

'Good of you,' she said scathingly.

He lowered his head, until it stopped inches from her own. Secretly pleased by her returning smart attitude. A sign she was feeling better. 'But that baby you're carrying so beautifully is mine too, and as both a parent and a doctor I cannot leave you here by yourself. Tell me what I can do to help?'

'Perhaps I should sit down for a moment,' she conceded.

Leo glanced around for a bench or wall low enough to sit on. 'I'm not sure there's anywhere suitable. Would you be willing to sit in the passenger seat of my car until you're ready to catch the bus?'

After a few seconds, she agreed. 'Okay.'

With care Leo led her over to his vehicle, unlocking it before opening the passenger's door to help her down onto the leather seat.

'Why are you doing this?' she asked, pushing the large giraffe at him to take.

'Because you need help.'

'Of course,' she muttered, not covering the bitterness in her tone. 'Why else? It isn't as though you care for me, is it? I'm just the dispensable wife. The woman good enough to impregnate, yet not come after.'

Leo flinched at her words, but this wasn't the time to correct her assumptions concerning their marriage and his true feelings for her. Soon the time would come for their inevitable heart-to-heart, despite what she said. But getting Gila home tonight so she could rest mattered more.

'Now tell me again what happened,' he gently quizzed.

She huffed, but answered, 'I told you, I became dizzy.'

'Has it happened before?' he asked, concerned that her midwife had somehow missed a problem with Gila's health and well-being.

She gave him a wry glance. 'Back off, Leo. You're not the only medical expert here. It's nothing to be concerned about. All my fault for rushing around when I'm so far along in the pregnancy.'

'How's your blood pressure?'

'Usually fine when I'm not bumping into ex-husbands,' she relied tartly.

'I know you may wish differently, but I am still your husband and both your and the baby's health are important to me.'

'My husband in name but nothing else,' she replied.

'You left me, remember,' he reminded her. 'Not the other way around.'

Leaning into the car, Leo opened the glove compartment and retrieved a bottle of water. Unscrewing the sealed cap, he handed it over. 'Drink this.'

Without complaint she took the bottle from him and took a small sip. After a few seconds, she took another. 'I really need to go.'

'A few more moments won't hurt. Stay there and rest.' He ached to touch her. To lay his hand upon her skin and breathe in her scent. The sweet exclusive one, that no beauty company or perfumer could recreate, because it was Gila's natural aroma. The very essence of the woman she was. As individual and unique as she. Just another thing he loved about her.

But his love or desires were no longer relevant. He'd lost the right to do any of the things he used to do. Their relationship no longer close or intimate.

For the last few months he'd fought other demons, but now he faced the shredded scraps of their marriage with no idea how to piece together a new kind of relationship between them from the fragmented remains.

'Is there anything else I can get you?' he asked softly. 'Something to eat, perhaps? The mini market is just over there.'

Gila glanced towards the shop across the street and groaned.

'What's wrong?'

'I'm pretty sure my bus just pulled away from the stop.' She sighed, her unusual show of vulnerability returning. 'I just want to go home and sink into a bath.'

Leo nodded, searching her face. Seeing again the tiredness in her pretty features. Gila needed to rest. 'Then let me drive you home.'

Amazingly, she stopped arguing and gave in. Giving Leo a stronger indication of how exhausted she really was, and a clue that perhaps the dizzy spell had frightened his normally resilient wife.

'Okay, but only because carrying the giraffe and my bag would be awkward on the bus and slightly embarrassing.'

He smiled and stood. He deposited the giraffe on the rear seat, a stirring of hope whispering through him for the first time in months.

When he'd first set eyes on Gila two years before, she'd been crouched in front of a young woman in the latter stages of giving birth in the unexpected surroundings of the hospital waiting area. While people around them had panicked and fussed, Gila had taken the woman's hands and calmly helped her through the birth, aware that any chance to get the patient into a birthing room or on a bed had long gone.

He had fallen in love with Gila that afternoon. But none of that mattered right now. Today the only thing that concerned him was getting Gila home to rest and making sure the baby was okay. Tomorrow could take care of everything else.

CHAPTER THREE

HOME SWEET HOME.

Gila managed to scramble inelegantly out of the car moments after Leo parked in the small residents' car park situated not far from the back street canal. She didn't want or need any assistance from him, well, no more than she'd already accepted, anyway.

Sitting beside him during the twenty-minute drive had turned into a form of emotional and physical torture. Every second fighting the urge to reach out and lay her hand upon his arm and gather strength and reassurance from the muscle beneath. Wanting to slide her fingers over the curve of his thigh and feel the heat coming through the material of his age-worn jeans.

'I would have helped you,' Leo said, rounding the car's bonnet and coming to a halt next to her. But Gila ignored him. As an independent woman, she needed no one. Hadn't she always known that? Hadn't life always indicated that to rely on others was nothing but a mistake that led to regret and disenchantment?

'I can manage,' she murmured, opening the back door to retrieve the oversized giraffe, suddenly craving the comfort of its soft squidgy body. Straightening, she slammed the door and waited for Leo to move out of the way, not inclined to give in over anything else. No matter how trivial or unimportant.

'Okay,' he said, backing off.

Her back ached and her shoes hurt. All she craved was a bath, a bowl of ice cream and a good weep. In exactly that order.

Shaking her head, she shoved past Leo, heading along the narrow, cobbled lane that led down to the canal that ran along the city's hidden back streets. Edged on both sides by a short, wide strip of forest, despite being so close to the hustle and bustle of busy London, it gave a tranquillity of calm that few in the city were privileged to live near to or experience.

Situated behind a row of expensive terrace houses in an area history once deemed a slum, this canal and many others had kept London and its many thriving businesses running during the industrial period. Separated from the houses by the high brick wall that ran along the bottom of the properties' small gardens.

These days the canal mostly accommodated holidaymakers and permanent residents who lived in the brightly decorated narrowboats. Just as Gila had since she turned fourteen years old and moved in with her uncle Art after her father became unable to care for her.

'Gila, will you please stop being so—?' Leo protested, hurrying after her.

She stopped, suddenly ready for a fight if it was the only way to get rid of him, and demanded, 'So what?'

He sucked in a breath, before replying, 'Nothing. I just want to make things better between us before the baby comes.'

To her shock and shame, she answered with a frustrated and irritable growl. Like something a bear cub would make.

Leo blinked twice, before asking, 'Did you just growl at me?'

Not wanting to admit to such odd behaviour, she swung around and stormed away. When had she started to growl at people? Was this a pregnancy thing, or a dumped and abandoned wife trait? Was she tumbling down the precarious tunnel of a disgruntled crazy ex? And was this only the start of such erratic behaviour?

Deciding not to dwell on the strange growling, Gila fixed her attention on the narrowboat moored up ahead. Finally, she stood close to her destination and a fridge with the tub of vanilla ice cream she'd been fantasising about for the last few hours. A handful of steps away from her home.

Home?

She took in the muddy brown painted narrowboat and silently sneered at the notion that this space was home. It wasn't. Not any more. In truth, not for some time. Not since the day she and Leo had moved in together.

Her eyes slowly and reluctantly slid to another narrowboat moored a few feet away, lovingly painted in a cheerful lilac colour with small pale blue wooden shutters. She let out a small sigh of pleasure at the heart-shaped cut-outs in the centre of each shutter. Ones Leo had handcrafted last year during one lazy summer afternoon. Baskets of orange and blue winter pansies sat on the roof and pink primroses mingled with purple heathers planted in traditionally painted barge ware buckets sat beside them.

When the narrowboat moored next to her uncle's had come up for sale several months before their wedding, she and Leo had jumped at the chance to buy it. House prices in the area were crazy and Gila had known she would miss the friendly community of friends and neighbours she had found since moving in with her uncle as a child. This place was more than just somewhere to live. Luckily Leo hadn't cared as long as she felt happy and settled. Yes, space was limited and the practicalities of everyday living on a narrowboat could be different from those of a house, especially once the baby arrived, but she didn't require a home full of furniture and filled with belongings she rarely used. Life on the narrowboat was simpler. And where else could you be so close to nature?

She glanced once more at the lilac narrowboat. That was her *real* home. The home she and Leo had so lovingly renovated from an unloved shell. Where they had spent their wedding night and subsequent months of their marriage, cocooned in their love and happiness until it all fell apart and collapsed. Their so-called wonderful relationship in truth an unstable construction built from rotten material and false dreams. Unable to withstand the first major hit life struck against them.

A time before Leo's sister, Jodie, took a fatal overdose of drugs and through her death destroyed Gila's marriage, too. Before Leo did nothing to prevent all they were from becoming waste and dust. Or perhaps the splinters had already been present in their marriage, hidden and ignored, but under the pressure of Jodie's demise they grew and widened leaving nothing but shattered hopes and spoilt wishes.

'I'll see you inside,' Leo offered. She nodded, figuring he simply wanted to do his duty and then leave for a date or something. She'd noted he popped out a couple of times a week when he wasn't working. Not that she'd purposely been spying. She certainly wasn't some estranged wife stalker, desperate to know her husband's every move. She didn't care where he went or what he did, she'd simply noticed that he went out two evenings a week for about an hour. Maybe he'd chosen to move on, even though they'd only split up a few months before. But time didn't matter to some men, did it? He worked with plenty of nurses and doctors who'd all be willing to give him comfort and understanding over a failed marriage.

Not that she cared. She didn't. Not really. What Leo did in his spare time was his prerogative. Just as if she wanted to date a million men, then she could. But no man was asking her out. And she might not be living with her husband any longer, but she still felt married. The stupid white band on her finger from where the sun had never got through her wedding ring still marked her as someone's partner. She still used her married name, too. She still felt like Mrs Gila Wright.

'I'd prefer you didn't,' she replied, not unkindly, but wearily. She couldn't stand any further time together. Not at this minute when the lonesomeness stung stronger than ever. Sitting next to him in the car had been hard enough, without him entering and invading her last small refuge. If he came inside the narrowboat, his presence would taint the area and leave her imagining him standing in a certain spot or sitting on a certain chair for the next few hours.

'Gila, we need to talk sometime. Please, just give me a date and a time. That is all I ask,' Leo persisted.

When hell became a favourite holiday destination, she almost replied. Why did they need to talk? She quite liked not talking. Why wasn't communicating through electronic impersonal means, each rigidly sticking to the subject of their baby and nothing else, enough for him? Besides, weren't brief, impersonal emails and texts better than the arguing they'd pursued for weeks after his sister's death? When the realisation that Leo wasn't just grieving, but slowly and determinedly shutting her out, had become clear.

Not talking didn't move their relationship backwards or forwards. It kept it stagnant. She wasn't ready or prepared for any new changes. Did he have a reason for suddenly wanting to talk? Like another woman? Was that behind his desire to converse? Had he met someone and wished to finish with his old life before moving on with a new one?

She shook the thought away. Nothing mattered but preparing for the arrival of their child. She didn't want to think about what Leo wanted or what he considered important. She wanted to be left alone with peace and quiet.

'Not today, Leo,' she said. 'I'm tired and all I want to do is lie on my bed and rest.'

'Are you taking enough iron?' He asked the same question she'd asked Reese earlier. 'You're very pale.'

'You're not my doctor,' she reminded him, all too aware she was every bit eight months pregnant and showing it in all ways. Not all of them appealing or attractive.

'I care—' he began, but stopped when she glared at him.

'But not enough, Leo,' she said, stepping onto the narrowboat. 'In the end, you proved that you didn't care enough, didn't you?'

'That is not true, Gila. Let me explain—'

She moved forward, but her foot caught on a piece of wood and she stumbled. Two arms wrapped around her from behind, pulling her into a close embrace. A stupid, traitorous part of her soul desperately yearned to lean back into the warmth of Leo's hard front, but the pain of the last few months and the way he'd shut her out returned to mock her. Silently questioning what the heck she was doing.

When she'd packed her bags, she had hoped the extreme action would shock Leo from the numb state he'd slumped into after his sister's death. Instead, he continued to live alone on their narrowboat, while she stayed on her uncle's. The gap already present between them broadening with each passing day. Leo had done nothing to show that he wanted her. Absolutely nothing.

And for the first time since they'd met, Gila had finally faced the cold harsh truth that while she loved Leo with every part of her heart and soul, he obviously didn't feel the same. Why else had he left her alone? What other possible reason could there be to explain why he mentally and physically did nothing to save their marriage?

'Let me check you over,' Leo said, helping Gila onto the small green sofa pushed against one wall. Bright yellow and green velvet cushions sat in each corner. Reaching behind, he tugged one from its place and propped it behind her back, then, with gentle fingers, pushed her against its softness and straightened.

'I'm fine,' she insisted, flustered by his caring manner. She didn't want him here or for him to see how sparse the narrowboat was despite the fact she'd been living there for weeks. When she'd left their home, she'd taken one small suitcase of clothes and nothing else. None of her silver thimble collection or the small assortment of art deco vases Leo had bought her over the months. Other than a few throws and some cushions, she'd not bothered to create much of a home. Initially, because she'd honestly believed her stay would be short-term. Then, when it had become clear that Leo no longer wanted her and their marriage, she'd lacked the energy to care about her surroundings. Besides, she doubted her uncle would be pleased if he returned from his six months touring wineries in France to find his home redecorated in soft and feminine colours. As a diehard bachelor he'd probably keel over from a coronary.

'It won't hurt to make sure, will it?' Leo said, ignoring her complaints.

'I'm sure you're busy,' she remarked, again attempting to get him to go.

He stared down at her, his mouth a flat, determined line. 'You and our child will always top anything else I am doing or have planned.'

She sighed and rested her hands on the top of her bump. Was he avoiding giving any hint to his plans for the evening, or was that just her suspicious mind? 'You really don't have to—'

'I do,' he insisted, cutting her off. 'I'll just go home and fetch my medical bag. It won't hurt to check your blood pressure.'

With a huff, she pointed to a plastic box in one corner. 'There's a sphygmomanometer in there you can use.'

Leo nodded and fetched the blood pressure kit and a stethoscope from the box.

Gila glanced around, her gaze falling on the toy giraffe now sitting on a small stool across the other side of the room. Was she imagining it, or was the stuffed toy grinning at her?

Crouching in front of her again, Leo said, 'Stop sulking.'

'I'm not sulking,' she denied, giving the giraffe one last look.

He smirked but let the subject drop. Instead, he wrapped the cuff around her arm, and asked, 'How often are you losing your balance and feeling dizzy?'

'That's the first time I've stumbled, but the dizzy spells are on and off. They only last for a few seconds, though. You know as well as I do that it happens sometimes in pregnancy. I've spoken to my midwife about it.'

'Good.' He pumped air into the cuff, before slowly releasing it, using the stethoscope to listen to her pulse. After a few seconds, he mused, 'Your blood pressure is a little raised.'

'I know. I check it regularly at the clinic. It's to be expected. My midwife feels it's nothing to be concerned with.'

'Even so. A few days of rest and relaxation will probably do you good.' He glanced up and searched her face. 'You look tired, Gila.'

'Thanks. I'm pregnant, what do you expect?' she grumbled, not in the mood to hear comments on her terrible appearance. Especially from a man who made most of the male population seem dull. She certainly wasn't going to admit she rarely slept through the night either. Not when dreams of him were mainly the reason.

'I'm not being unkind,' he said, but stopped when she glanced away. Instead, he asked, 'Do you have the weekend off?'

'Yes,' she said, then frowned. 'Look, you can go now. I'm feeling fine.'

He removed the cuff and dropped it onto the sofa. After asking her several further questions, he leaned back on his heels.

'I only have a few days left to work at the clinic,' she said, hopeful that there might be a way for them both to work there without her needing to give up before she intended. 'Can we at least agree to keep out of each other's way?'

'Is that what you want?' he asked quietly.

She forced every emotion, doubt and disappointment burning inside her not to show on her face. Desperate to hide the fact that having him this near broke her heart all over again. 'Of course.'

He sighed and stood. Returning the sphygmomanometer and stethoscope to the box, he headed for the entrance.

At the door, he turned back. 'That's not just your child you're carrying, remember? It's ours.'

'Get out,' she choked, too furious to say

more. Leo needed to go before she grabbed every small object in the room and threw them at him. How dared he? He'd caused the breakdown of their relationship, yet he dared to stand there as though he were in some way the injured one. She'd made a point to keep him informed on the baby's development and welfare during the last four months, when plenty of other women wouldn't have bothered. Keen to show that her baby's needs and happiness would always be her priority, even if it meant involving him. She loved her child. Real heart-thumping love and not the kind that disappeared under pressure.

'Get out!' she repeated, through clenched teeth, already knowing it would be hours before she could breathe without taking in the familiar smell of his damn lingering aftershave. 'Just, get out!'

Leo shut the wooden doors and stepped onto the narrowboat's deck. Stepping off and onto the path that ran along the canal, he glanced up at the sound of approaching footsteps, his heart sinking at the sight of the old man marching along the same lane he and Gila had used only minutes before. Could this afternoon deteriorate any further? Not only a stupid row with Gila, but now her uncle's unexpected return.

'Leo.' Art stopped several steps away. Both his tone and expression neutral and friendly. But Leo wasn't fooled. Art Brown had raised Gila for a good part of her childhood and they shared a close relationship. The man was as protective as any birth parent. 'Have you and my niece finally made amends?'

Leo shoved his hands into his jeans pockets. With a long glance at the narrowboat, he shook his head. 'No. Let's just say negotiations are still hostile.'

'Oh,' Art murmured, following it with a heavy sigh.

Leo decided to change the subject, not seeing any point in raking over a situation that wasn't about to change soon. 'You should know, Gila recently experienced a funny turn at the clinic where she volunteers. I brought her home and checked her over, but she needs to rest. Perhaps you can convince her to take it easy for the next couple of days.'

'You happened to be at the clinic, did you?' Art asked, his expression curious. 'Lucky you were there to help when she needed it.'

Leo shrugged, not about to get into the hows and whys of his attendance at the clinic. Dr Peters's family business wasn't for broadcasting to everyone. He just hoped the man reached the States in time to see his grandchild. The accident and injuries she'd suffered were severe and life-threatening. Personally, he thought the prognosis wasn't good.

Art's gaze slid to the narrowboat they stood beside. 'I guess Gila's home. I need to speak to her.'

'Yes,' he confirmed, before moving to leave, but Art stopped him.

'You might want to join us.'

Surprised by the invitation, Leo shook his head and declined. 'I doubt Gila will appreciate my presence considering she's just ordered me to leave. We've had a row of sorts. I said the wrong thing.'

Art chuckled. 'Yeah, well, sometimes we men do that. The truth is, Leo, you may be interested in what I have to say.'

After a few seconds, Leo followed Art onto the narrowboat. Not looking forward to his wife's reaction, he hung back. Whatever the reason for Art's return, he wasn't sure he wanted to get involved and risk upsetting Gila more.

CHAPTER FOUR

'ART!'

Gila shifted on the sofa and pushed to her feet as warmth and surprise bubbled through her. The last thing she'd expected after Leo's departure was for her uncle to appear within minutes. But she was glad he had, because she needed the man's kindness and comfort right now.

She smiled as her uncle crossed the small space and grabbed both her hands, planting a noisy kiss to her knuckles, in the same way he'd always done since Gila was a child.

'Goodness, you've grown bigger in certain places since I last saw you,' he teased, drawing her back down onto the sofa and taking a seat next to her. He smiled at her very round and obvious baby bump, before gently resting an aged hand upon it. 'Looking gorgeous, sweetheart.'

Her smile bloomed into a full grin. No matter how low she felt, whenever her uncle was close, he always put brightness into her day and filled her with love. Something definitely lacking from her life for some time. 'Yeah, well, a growing baby isn't one of those things you can really hide.'

Art laughed and silently regarded her. 'You really are beautiful,' he complimented. 'Isn't she, Leo? Pregnancy never looked so good on a woman.'

Gila frowned and glanced from her uncle to find Leo once more standing across the small space. Arms crossed, he leaned against the kitchen opening. He nodded in answer to her uncle's question, his gaze slowly dropping to rest on her bump. The optical trace an invisible caress that left her skin and nerves tingling.

'Yes, she is,' he finally replied.

Her heart squeezed at his words, but she ignored her body's disloyal reactions and turned her full attention to her uncle. The confidence bash of a failed marriage had left her feeling unattractive and undesirable, yet the sensation of Leo's intense gaze dispersed all those feelings and left something very different pacing through her body. A feeling she reluctantly liked.

Ignoring the man across the room, she stared

at her uncle, noticing how happy, healthy and relaxed he looked. His tour around France had obviously done him good, though the fact he'd returned early was concerning.

'I thought you planned to return to England at the end of June,' she said, hoping there wasn't anything wrong. He'd suffered a small health scare the year before, but nothing that wasn't easily treated and cured.

'I did, but an unexpected situation has cropped up and changed my plans,' Art answered, his fingers slipping away from hers.

A shiver of apprehension tickled along Gila's spine and for a moment the old, dreaded sensation she remembered from her childhood returned. When her father would utter similar remarks before dropping a bombshell into their already chaotic life. His idea of childcare invariably involved carting Gila off to unknown places, often with newly met acquaintances, with little thought to stability or adequate schooling.

Her lone parent had fallen in and out of love with the ease and regularity of a passing season. Gila was the result of one of those doomed love affairs. Her mother had disappeared out of their lives before Gila was six months old and never returned. Though having a small daughter never curbed her father's natural inclination to drift from one relationship to another, or to travel from country to country. She'd lost count of the many homes and cities they'd briefly lived in. Sometimes invited and legally, other times not so. He'd liked to call himself a free spirit, whereas others had labelled him an unreliable and incompetent parent.

'What's wrong, Art?' Without meaning to, she shifted her gaze to Leo. Was her uncle ill? Was her estranged husband here to ease the sharing of bad news? What did Leo know that she didn't? Were the pair keeping secrets from her?

Art sighed, his fingers claiming hers again. With a slight squeeze, he said, 'I need to come home, darling girl. To the narrowboat.'

'What?' she gasped. What did he mean? Was he home for good? If so, that was wonderful, but they'd shared the space while she was growing up, so she didn't understand his words or his serious manner. As though he feared telling her more.

'I have something of an emergency—'

'What emergency?' she demanded, preventing him from finishing. 'Are you sick again?'

'No, no, nothing like that,' he soothed, patting her hands. 'You see, I've met a woman called Maggie.'

'Oh,' she said, her heart sinking as that much despised awareness crept through stronger at the mention of this stranger. It and the happy glint in her uncle's eyes. 'And?'

'She was part of the group I toured the wineries with. She's a lovely lady. You'll love her. The thing is we've come back early because she needs to have an operation, but she's not allowed to travel home to Devon straight away. Something about needing to see the specialist afterwards. The hospital had a cancellation and brought the date for her operation forward. Anyway, she needs a place to stay. It's only for a week, and I would like to help her. She really is a wonderful woman and we've become very close over the weeks in France.'

Gila couldn't believe what Art was saying. While one part of her was pleased to see how happy her uncle was, she couldn't help wondering how they were all going to live on the narrowboat when there were only two small bedrooms. 'Couldn't Maggie stay at a hotel?'

'Not really. She hasn't much money and it's only for a week,' Art insisted. 'I'm sure we can manage. Maggie can sleep in my room and I'll sleep on the sofa. She's very funny and I'm certain you'll get on.'

Three people living in the tight confines of her uncle's narrowboat, which was smaller than the one she'd shared with Leo, would be snug. Having to spend time around two very cheerful and, from the silly smile on Art's face every time he spoke about this Maggie, loved-up people sounded dreadful even if it was only for a week.

'Perhaps I can find a hotel room,' she suggested, determined to find an alternative. 'Though with it being Easter weekend it might be hard to find somewhere with a free room.'

'You can move back in with me, if you want,' Leo quietly offered. 'It's only for a week. You're right—all the hotels will be fully booked with tourists and people attending the sports event that's taking place in the city on Saturday.'

'No, thank you,' Gila refused, not interested in the offer. She would *not* go back to the narrowboat they'd once shared. How could he suggest such a thing? She'd find somewhere else to stay. Not that she could really afford the expense of a hotel room for a week, not when she still needed to buy a couple of expensive items for the baby.

'I should probably mention that Maggie is arriving tonight. I'm collecting her from the train station in an hour. She wanted to pop home to Devon first and collect some extra belongings.'

'I see,' Gila said, shocked by the short notice her uncle was giving her to find alternative accommodation. It wasn't as if she could call a friend for a favour, because she had purposely kept quiet over the break-up with Leo.

'I should leave,' Leo said. 'You two need to discuss this on your own. Just let me know if you change your mind and want to stay with me, Gila.'

Art stood and nodded. 'It was good to see you, Leo.'

'And you.' Leo glanced at Gila, and asked, 'Are you okay?'

No, she wasn't. She wanted everything to go back to how it was a few months before. But fairy tales were for children and she'd never bothered to trust in them anyway. Had always known they were nothing but a fantasy created by adults. What she wanted to do was crawl into bed and not get out again until she'd dreamed a life where fathers, uncles and husbands didn't repeatedly let her down. 'Yes, I'm fine.'

Art waited until Leo's footsteps sounded on the path outside the narrowboat, before turning to Gila. 'I'm sorry about the short notice, but I'm sure we can manage for a week.'

Seven long days playing gooseberry to her uncle and this mysterious new woman he was so taken with. No, thanks. She'd prefer not to be an up-close spectator of her uncle's love life. 'No, it's fine. I'll find somewhere else and give you both some space.'

Her uncle stared at her for several moments, before he gently asked, 'Honey, why are you still here?'

She sighed. 'I told you on the phone. I've left Leo.'

'But why? I know things became tough after his sister died, but to leave the man when he was grieving.'

She stiffened. 'You make it sound like I wanted to.'

Art tilted his head to one side. 'When you were a child and you found life at home too hard, what did you always do?'

She shrugged and lied. 'I can't remember.'

'You used to run away,' Art said. 'Always hid here until I found you. Seems to me, you did the same thing this time. Trouble was Leo didn't come to find you, did he?'

Gila's lips trembled and she whispered, 'He

didn't even come knocking on the door. And I left him a note telling him where I was.'

Tugging Gila gently to him, Art kissed her forehead. 'You need to stop running away when things are hard or scary. You're a beautiful, wonderful woman, who needs to learn to stand your ground and demand better whenever you're upset with life or people.'

'I thought if I left him he would realise how bad everything had become between us. I kept asking him how I could help, but he just refused to talk to me.' She turned her face into her uncle's shoulder. 'He didn't love me enough to come after me, Art. He didn't even try.'

'You sure?'

'I'm still here, aren't I?' Waiting and lonely. Wondering what else she could have done and what it was about her that made her so unlovable.

'I'm not saying the man hasn't acted like an idiot,' Art said. 'He has. But sometimes life is hard work and people…people you love do things you don't understand.'

'Don't you think I already know that?'

'This situation with Leo is not the same, kid. Your husband is not your father.'

'Isn't he? He's let me down too, hasn't he? Just the same as Dad.'

'Did he or did you just expect too much from someone who was in the worst kind of agony? And believe me grief is no easy gig to come out from. I've suffered a long spell there myself.'

It wasn't often her uncle mentioned the woman he'd loved and lost many years ago. A woman who died too young. Before medicine had advanced enough to help her. 'I don't know.'

'Honey, Leo isn't going to go away. For the next eighteen years at least he's going to be in and out of your life. You two need to come to a decision on how to share your child's future and upbringing.'

'And then what?' she asked, almost frightened to hear Art's reply.

'Move on and rebuild. But between you and Leo, that child you're growing deserves a safe and happy childhood. With parents who can be civil to each other. At some point, I'm afraid, you're going to have to face that.'

Gila snatched the pink jumper from the bed and threw it into the bag, along with the rest of her hastily packed clothes.

This morning when she'd rolled, literally, out of bed, her concerns had amounted to whether she could get through the day without thinking about her marriage or manage an hour without the desire to empty her bladder. Now she faced not only the idea of seeing her estranged husband at work, but also that for the next week she was homeless.

Okay, perhaps not exactly homeless, but almost as bad. Though being homeless did come with the bonus of being able to choose whose company you kept. She'd spent the last half an hour searching the Internet for nearby hotels with a free room, but every single one was full. Leaving her with no choice, for tonight at least, but to accept Leo's offer rather than stay here and suffer the discomfort of being the spare part to a happy couple. And the sofa was just too old and uncomfortable for her seventy-five-year-old uncle to sleep on.

Plonking down onto the bed, she lowered her head, squeezing her eyes shut as the weight of the forthcoming situation engulfed her. Not only was she going back to the lovely home she and Leo had shared, but the close confinement and situation would necessitate time in each other's company. Close periods together, which was fine if they liked and loved one another, but when their relationship was strained and in pieces, the idea sounded horrific.

As if she didn't already have enough stress in her life, wondering over the future, without this added complication. Seven days with a man who'd made it clear he didn't love her.

Standing, Gila grabbed the bag. The same one she'd used the night she'd left Leo when she'd still clung to the hope of salvaging her relationship. What a fool she'd been to hope for a positive resolution. Instead of the loving reunion she'd wished for, she and Leo had shifted from not talking, to only conversing over the baby and its needs. She guessed she should be grateful he still showed an interest in their child, even if he no longer cared for *her*.

Leaving the bedroom, she made her way through the narrowboat. Her uncle had disappeared, no doubt to let Leo know she had no choice but to move back in with him, before heading to the station to collect Maggie.

Walking the short distance to Leo's narrowboat, Gila concentrated on slowing down her suddenly erratic breathing. Perhaps the nervous buzzing in her stomach was indigestion due to the baby? The whole situation certainly soured her mood, so why not her stomach?

With a shake of her head, Gila stopped and drew in a deep breath, her gaze returning to the lilac narrowboat. What was the matter with her? Seven days wasn't so long, really. And a hotel room might become free before that. She intended to check the hotel sites each day just in case. With luck she and Leo would aim to avoid one another as much as possible. With his shifts at the clinic and the hospital, and her last two days volunteering, it shouldn't be too hard. And on his day off, she'd make herself scarce. Go into the city and visit a museum or two. Enjoy lunch at a local restaurant. She still needed to shop for the baby, and she also had an appointment with her midwife next week. Yes, with so many things to do, they'd hardly see each other. She'd make sure of it.

Maybe she could use the time to finally call an end to her marriage for good. Spend the next few days letting go so she could move on with the rest of her life. Build a new base for their future relationship. One that saw them putting their child before anything else. Before each other. Surely that wouldn't be too hard?

Her uncle was right. It didn't matter whether it was hard or not. It was how things were going to be and something they were going to have to do. Better to start by making that clear to Leo. They might no longer be lovers in any sense, but they would soon be co-parents, after all.

It was also time to stop acting like a naive, trusting fool and admit that, where relationships were concerned, the rainbows quickly disappeared and left nothing but oily puddles. And never again would she be stupid enough to fall for a so-called handsome hero. Not now she knew they truly didn't exist.

Gila's stomach tensed as she stepped onto the narrowboat and caught sight of a small wooden heart nailed above the two wooden doors that led inside. A pathetic lump of heartache mixed with fury destroyed all her freshly made decrees. Ignoring the burn in her chest, she reached for the door handle.

For over a year this had been her first true home. Hers and Leo's. Their love nest, as they'd fondly named it. Where they'd shared their first night together, yelled through their first argument and kissed beneath the stars on their wedding night, desperate to be alone after a wonderful day surrounded by friends and family. And where the child she now carried was lovingly and passionately conceived.

Despite the passing weeks since she'd last stepped onto the boat, an odd and unexpected sense of homecoming threaded stronger around all the other emotions humming through her. Surely time apart should've changed how she viewed this place and what it once represented? Given her a better clarity on her marriage, instead of this sudden swell of aching regrets and yearnings.

Stepping down the narrow steps into the tiny kitchen, she was shocked to find none of the mess or disorder she'd anticipated. A secret part had imagined Leo falling to pieces without her. Obviously, just another thing she'd been mistaken about.

She moved into the small, but welcoming lounge, her nerves easing at the sight of the familiar soft chalky blue walls and the teal velvet Chesterfield sofa. With a quick scan around, she noted everything was as she'd left it. Why she'd half expected changes, she didn't know, but the odd buzzing inside her stomach started to settle.

Passing through this room, too, she only stopped when she reached the bedroom. Leo stood inside, gathering several items of clothing from a small chest of drawers. He glanced up when she hovered in the open doorway.

'Art's spoken to you?' she asked.

He nodded. 'Yeah.'

'As soon as I find somewhere else to stay—' she started to explain.

'It's fine. Stay as long as you want. I'll sleep on the sofa,' he said, picking up a blue woollen jumper and adding it to the items already hanging over one arm. He glanced meaningfully at her bump and smiled softly. 'You need the bed far more than I do.'

'I don't want to inconvenience you,' she said, in two minds over whether sleeping in the bed they once shared was a good idea. But slumming on the sofa didn't appeal as an alternative, either. These days she found it hard to get comfy wherever she slept. Besides, Leo had regularly fallen into a contented sleep on the sofa in the past, so he'd probably be fine. 'I'm sure I can manage for a week.'

'No, you need a comfortable bed. You won't get enough sleep on the sofa. Besides, the bed is every bit as much yours as it is mine. You discovered it in that old antique shop, remember?'

Memories of that day wandering around the nearby antiques centre floated through her mind. Pure art deco in every straight line and angle of the old bed, she'd fallen in love with it the moment she'd seen it. In excitement, she'd phoned Leo at work and sent photographs. Within minutes, he'd agreed it was ideal and Gila had made the seller an offer. They hadn't worried about how they'd fit the large bedframe into the narrowboat's cramped bedroom space. They'd just known they had to own it.

Leo finished collecting his belongings and moved to slip past where she still hesitated on the threshold. How easy it would be to reach out and slowly run her fingertips over the contours of his T-shirt. Rest her palm flat in the centre of his chest and experience the steady dull thud of his heartbeat against her hand. How she longed to lean her head against his shoulder and breathe in the scent of the one place in the world she'd ever felt completely safe and secure.

How effortless it would be to indulge herself in what they once were, but she couldn't do that. Just as she refused to forget the painful, empty weeks they'd been apart. Or the events that led to her departure. How he'd allowed the horrid wordless stalemate in their marriage to become bigger than anything else. So huge and dominant that it drove her from their home.

Home. That annoying word again. A fantasy she had spent most of her life without.

'Please, just make yourself at home,' he offered politely.

Wondering if her thoughts had shown on

her face, she snapped, 'But it's not my home. Not any more.'

A gigantic lie, considering the contentment soothing into her soul since returning.

If she'd slapped him across the face, Gila doubted the impact would have been as robust. The shutters in Leo's eyes returned and closed her out. Those same much-hated shutters she'd seen so often during those last weeks before she left. Barring her from his internal thoughts and feelings, only this time she didn't blame him. Her remark was both cruel and unnecessary, and she hated how it sent him into retreat.

'I need to go out,' Leo said, stepping away. 'I've a meeting and a patient to check. I'll see you tonight, unless you're already in bed.'

'I will be,' she said, her eyes drifting again to the bed. The one they'd shared for over a year. Where they'd laughed and made love. Where they'd confessed secrets and shared Sunday morning tea mixed with buttered toast and laughter. The place where she'd believed they were their true selves. Where she'd sworn their love grew stronger.

And once again the overpowering sense of returning home caused another break in her already battered heart.

CHAPTER FIVE

GILA WOKE UP tired the following morning, having spent the night twisting and turning as best her bump would allow. Her back still ached, adding to her night of discomfort. Though, she wasn't convinced the main reason for her physical unsettledness came down to only lack of sleep. Knowing Leo lay a few feet away in the lounge didn't help her peace of mind.

Staring at the ceiling, she slid a hand tenderly over her child, alert to the sounds both outside and inside the narrowboat. Birdsong mingled with the occasional soft thump from the room next door, which indicated Leo was awake and getting ready for work. Going through his usual morning routine. When he'd returned last night, she'd still been up reading a book, and he'd mentioned having an early shift at the hospital.

Had he eaten his customary breakfast of

cereal drenched in milk before having his shower? Or had he changed his daily habits in the last four months? Formed new ones that she wouldn't know or recognise.

Sighing, Gila rolled onto her side, purposely diverting her thoughts from the man she spent too much time thinking about. If she didn't find some way to occupy herself over the next few days, she would go mad counting the hours and minutes before she could leave.

This was all her uncle's fault. And she had a feeling the fates and the universe were involved, too.

And what about Leo?

She sighed as her wandering mind returned to the man in the next room. What was she going to do about him? As much as she'd happily defer it to some time later, a decision did need to be made about the future. She'd purposely ignored the idea of a long-term separation and the hassle of organising a divorce, but he said he wanted to talk, to explain things. What things? And did she really care any more? The past couldn't be erased and changed. So what was the point?

She opened her eyes and silently repeated the dreaded word. Divorce. Such an ugly-sounding term. She didn't really want one.

When she'd uttered her vows to love, honour and cherish, she'd meant them for life. But only an obstinate idiot held onto a broken relationship. And she might be a fool, but she refused to be a totally hopeless one.

With a divorce came arguing over possessions and money. Wrangling over who got what and why. So far, they had sidestepped both subjects. All interaction they'd shared for the last few months had centred only on their unborn child. If she shifted the focus to include more practical, home-life stuff, then she would need to think about where she wanted to live and that all sounded like too much work right now.

Art's words from last night filtered through her thoughts. She didn't need a week to sort out her true feelings for Leo. She no longer had any. Well, okay, she did still experience anger and frustration, but that was to be expected, wasn't it? And those feelings were because of how stupid she felt, not because of something more powerful. Absolutely nothing to do with bruised love or crushed ego.

No, she did *not* love Leo Wright. Not any more. Not for weeks, in fact. Where love had once beaten and grown, numbness now filled its hollow space.

She rolled over and shut her eyes. Perhaps

if she said the words with more gusto, they might sound more convincing? God, she truly was pathetic.

The too familiar pressure of her bladder became uncomfortable, giving her no other choice but to close down her internal reflections and rise from the bed. Pulling on her yoga outfit, she gave herself a quick pep talk and then grabbed her blue rubber yoga mat. With luck, Leo would be heading out soon and she could complete her morning's yoga stretches alone before her shower.

She groaned and left the room. The following days were going to be hell, she just knew it.

'Morning,' Leo greeted the second Gila stepped into the lounge. Forcing his feet not to move, he privately fought the temptation to race over and grab Gila in a bearhug. Kiss her full pretty mouth, the way he used to every morning. God, she looked so good standing in their home.

For the last few months, he'd missed seeing her every morning. Pined like a sad dog for the way she filled a room with her company just by stepping into it. His gaze ran over her, taking in the sleepy sheen to her eyes, the haphazard ponytail her hair was pulled into and the flushed rosy tinge to her cheeks. His gaze lowered, skimming down over the tight-fitting yoga top, boldly hugging her generous pregnancy curves until it settled on the large arch of her baby bump.

'You are...' His words trailed off as he dragged his gaze from her stomach and returned to her face. Smiling softly, he finished, 'Nothing, forget I spoke.'

He'd intended telling her she was beautiful, but he suspected she wouldn't appreciate the compliment and he didn't wish to see the sharp flash of pain and distrust the words would produce in her grey eyes. A simple compliment from him now had the power to hurt and offend her.

His stomach jerked and the never-ending rush of self-loathing returned for the irrational way he'd handled his sister's death, and the damage he'd allowed it to cause to his marriage. For the thoughtless and unintentional way he'd hurt Gila.

Gila waved the mat in her hands towards the floor, not acknowledging or questioning his comment. 'I need to do my morning stretches. I won't be long.'

He nodded and reluctantly finished his mug of cold tea. The last thing he wished to do was leave, but watching Gila in that outfit, while she ran through her morning workout, threatened to undo all the promises he'd made in the early hours while trying to get comfortable on the sofa. He refused to do anything to spook Gila into leaving before they talked. Not before he told her everything and exactly what he'd been doing for the last few months, when she imagined he'd done nothing but let their relationship go.

Taking a last sip of his drink, Leo murmured, 'I'll get out of your way. I'll probably be late tonight. I have to go somewhere after my shift.'

Gila kept her attention on performing her yoga sequence.

Leo grabbed his car keys, his attention sliding back to his wife as she quickly settled into a series of poses. Something he'd witnessed many times, yet today, with the changes to her body, it felt different. Like watching a familiar stranger. The grace and poise she exuded as she moved through each different position—the Tree, the Half Moon and his own personal favourite, the Cat-Cow, always fascinated him.

He smiled as she moved into the Warrior position, his humour turning to concern as she suddenly gasped and straightened. Slamming the mug down onto the worktop, he dropped his keys and was beside her within seconds. 'Are you okay? Can I help?'

She shook her head and stammered, 'I—I...'

Night and day, from a distance he'd observed her growing their child, hungry for the chance to touch Gila. To explore the changes of her new and unaccustomed shape and run his hands over the precious life developing inside her body. To reconnect in some small physical way with the woman who owned his soul and the child he didn't know.

But his hands stayed by his side where they now belonged. He'd lost the right to touch her months ago.

Gila stiffened and shuffled away. 'I'm okay, thanks. Just baby deciding to shift positions. I think I'll go shower now.'

Leo swallowed the burst of disappointment and nodded. He waited until she'd disappeared into the bathroom before letting out a shaky breath. Want and desire raced through him, mingling with intense pain. How was he going to mend things when she flinched away from his presence? How was he going to gain her forgiveness when he knew he didn't deserve it? He'd treated her badly after Jodie's death. He'd not acted cruelly or physically harmed her, but he had turned away from her love. Away from her and her concern. He didn't blame Gila for not wanting to let him close again. She had every right to mistrust him. To despise him for mentally locking her out.

He retrieved his discarded car keys from the floor, his hands still tingling from aching to touch the woman he loved. His heart heavy of all that he had lost. Somehow, he had to accomplish the impossible and prove to Gila that he'd never hurt her again or disappoint their child. Regain her trust. The problem was he didn't know if either one was even possible.

Leo parked his car outside the old city cemetery and strolled towards the large ornate black gates. His thoughts were troubled as he passed row after row of graves, many from the previous century, until he eventually reached a large marble angel.

This grave stood out amongst the weathered gravestones because of its newness. Lichen, weather and time had yet to age and mute it into its green and peaceful tree-lined surroundings.

Linking his hands, Leo bent his head for a moment, before his eyes moved to read the still bright gold lettering on the stone. His heart pinching hard at the sight of the name: *Jodie Margaret Wright*.

His kid sister. His only sibling, born twelve years after his own birth. A young woman he'd spent most of his life trying to protect from herself, and yet had failed atrociously when it really mattered.

Crouching, he brushed his fingertips tenderly over the name, similar to the way he once wiped away her childhood tears whenever life turned cruel.

'Hey, kid,' he said softly. 'How's it going in heaven? I bet you're giving all those saints a hard time, eh?'

He visited his sister's grave once a week since she'd taken her own life in a drugs and drink overdose. Once a bright, happy young woman determined to conquer the world and pursue her chosen path as a dancer.

But then a tragic accident had killed her boyfriend. A boy she'd grown up loving, and it had tipped her into the world of despair and drugs when she'd met a group of people who handed out narcotics like harmless snacks that wouldn't ruin her life and rob her of her precious dreams.

Instead of throwing herself into her career to soothe the pain, Jodie had slowly melted into the destruction of being an addict. Concerned only with her next high, rather than pirouetting across the world's dance stages.

The years of trying to get Jodie clean had been a nightmare. The worrying times she'd disappeared for weeks on end, then reappeared sick, staying in Leo's company long enough to steal items of value, before leaving again. A pattern that had gone on for years, until Leo had finally found the strength to stop it. To halt the never-ending repetition that had disrupted their lives.

Unable to cope with the shame of having a drug-addict daughter, his parents had moved away from the city to their villa in Spain several years before. Leaving Leo once again with the responsibility of his younger sibling.

When he'd met and married Gila, he'd purposely pulled away from his sister's problems and her destructive lifestyle, not wanting it to taint his and Gila's relationship. But Jodie had grown to resent Gila and had often caused trouble to the point where Leo had been forced to choose between them. Pushing him until in the end he'd chosen the woman he loved the most. Gila.

Two months later Jodie lay in this grave and for weeks the guilt of wondering if his rejection had pushed his unstable sister over the edge had consumed and hounded his every thought until he could barely think or act.

'Gila's come home,' he said quietly, rubbing his fingers across the angel on top of the headstone. Her shaped wing cold beneath his touch. Aware his sister would not share his happiness at the news. But he no longer cared. He wanted his wife and child back in his life in whatever arrangement Gila chose.

'She didn't want to come home,' he continued, his fingers pausing against the marble. 'But she has. I guess I'm preferable to a park bench.'

The sound of a jackdaw calling in the late afternoon answered his words and he smiled. 'I'm not going to mess things up this time, Jodie. I'm sorry I let you down and told you to stay away from my home, but I couldn't risk you around Gila. You'd become so unpredictable and when she became pregnant, I didn't trust you not to become angry and violent. If you'd ever hurt her or the baby...'

He swallowed hard, their last angry conversation replaying in his mind. When he'd made it clear to his sister that he would no longer put up with her demands for attention or money, he'd not said why, but she'd known Leo well enough to guess his reasons for forcing her away from his family.

By protecting his wife, Leo had failed his sister and it had taken him a long time to accept the responsibility of that decision. One he now understood and recognised as his only choice in the circumstances. To protect one female, he'd had no choice but to reject and hurt the other.

Reaching into his pocket, Leo withdrew a small crème Easter egg. Rubbing the pad of his thumb lightly over the pink foil wrapping, he crouched and positioned the egg onto the grave, pushing it gently into the soft soil.

'Happy Easter, Jodie. I hope you are happier in heaven than you ever were on earth.'

Straightening, he walked away, determined to fight for his relationship with his unborn child and for the friendship he used to share with his wife. The one thing he unthinkingly threw away and wanted back more than anything.

CHAPTER SIX

Gila shifted the floral bouquet and considered for the hundredth time whether a friendship could withstand a small let-down like bailing on an engagement party. But she knew if she didn't make an appearance, her friend Bea would insist on tracking Gila down, whether her fiancé minded or not. Though knowing the man, he'd probably be leading the needless search party.

In truth, she didn't want to celebrate anything, but she and Bea had been friends for years so, despite her reluctance, Gila didn't want to disappoint the other woman. Or hear the lecture she'd no doubt receive if she did bail. Besides, Gila figured she only needed to stay long enough to hand over the flowers, offer her congratulations and then disappear into the crowd before sneaking off home. Confident she wouldn't really be missed with so many other people to distract her friend's attention throughout the afternoon.

So here she stood at the entrance of a local restaurant's tiny outdoor garden area, searching through the sea of friends, relations and diners for sight of Bea and her wonderful fiancé, Nick.

Feeling unhospitable, though a common occurrence for Gila lately wasn't the main reason for her lack of enthusiasm for the get-together. Her reluctance for the occasion had more to do with the knowledge that she suspected Leo would arrive at some point during the afternoon, considering that Bea's fiancé also happened to be his best friend and that was enough to crush any of Gila's excitement and eagerness for the celebrations.

She and Leo had actually brought the couple together, when Bea and Nick had separately gatecrashed their third date. Their excuses, when they had turned up within minutes of each other, had been simply to check out their best friend's date, whom they had been sick and tired of hearing brilliant and unbelievable things about. Both long-time dating cynics, neither Bea nor Nick had believed such a fabulous person existed, or that their friend had been dating them. So they'd both arrived with the intention of finding fault with their best friend's new other half, and instead had found themselves drawn to each other. By the end of the evening they'd arranged to go on their own date the next night.

Gila sighed, frowning at the strong scent coming from the flowers. As if seeing Leo at home weren't hard enough. Seriously, she could do without constantly encountering the man outside the narrowboat and clinic, too. The last thing she felt inclined to do was spend the afternoon watching all the unmarried women gush around Leo once people learnt they were no longer together.

Despite her hostile attitude towards Leo, she couldn't deny his attraction. She'd fallen for his handsome looks on first sight and then toppled into love after one single conversation when his charming personality had totally floored her. Her uncle had insisted for years that when she met the right man she'd know. And she'd fallen for Leo like a storm-split tree crashing onto shaky and unknown ground. Full force and with a vibrating boom. He'd amazed her with his funny attitude to life and the sweet way he could tug a smile from her no matter what mood she was in or how bad her day.

'You came!' squealed a female voice from

across the garden, causing several people to jump and spill their drinks.

Startled from her musings, Gila chuckled as her best friend rushed from a group of guests to wrap her in an awkward hug. 'My God, the baby is growing huge. How on earth are you managing to lug it around?'

'The miracle of pregnancy.' She laughed, not offended by her friend's tactless remark. Bea was famous for speaking without thinking. The knack of saying what she thought without filtering or considering others' sensitivities just a part of her charm. 'Though sometimes I do wonder at it myself.'

Bea shifted and flicked a stern gaze over Gila's face. 'I fully expected you not to come. To find some flimsy excuse to sit at home and mope.'

'Me?' she quizzed innocently. Heat warmed her cheeks and gave her away, but she continued with her guiltless act. 'Why would I do that?'

'Because your delightful other half is here and I expect you to want to avoid him. When are you two going to sort yourselves out?'

'How do you like being engaged?' Gila asked, changing the subject, before she shoved the flowers into Bea's mouth to stop her talking. Couldn't she have a few hours where she didn't have to do a thing but enjoy herself? Was it really such a tough ask?

'Love it,' Bea replied, taking the bouquet from her. 'Now tell me the truth. How are things between you and Leo really? Come on, tell me. Do I need to get Nick to challenge him to something exciting and dangerous, the way they used to in the Regency period whenever a female was wronged by a man?'

'Pretty much the same as when you asked last week,' Gila replied, not about to inform her friend that she and Leo were once again sharing a home. Obviously Leo hadn't told Nick about the change so she wasn't going to. The last thing she wanted was for Bea to start imagining reunions and happy ever afters.

'Oh, Gila. I know he's a dolt, and you're hurt, but is there really no hope? I mean, let's admit the truth, men are on the whole pretty useless when it comes to the sharing and caring stuff—'

'Bea, don't,' Gila warned quietly.

'Okay, I'm being my usual insensitive self, aren't I? But it's only because I love you so much and want you happy. Would you like me to punch him hard on the arm next time I see him? Just like I used to with the mean boys at school when we were kids.'

Gila laughed and shook her head. 'I'm fine, honest.'

Bea let out a heavy sigh, then tensed. 'Prepare yourself, then. Leo's about to stroll by.'

Gila almost snatched the flowers back to use as a barricade between herself and Leo, but then sanity returned. The man would no doubt walk straight past. Nothing to worry over. If she just kept her head and acted relaxed and indifferent everything would be good.

'Bea,' Leo greeted, halting to stand beside them.

'Leo,' Bea greeted politely. 'If you're looking for Nick, he's inside playing darts with a cousin. How are you keeping?'

'I'm fine—'

'Bea, quick, Mum needs you.' Bea's teenage sister, Lola, joined them and started to drag Bea away. 'Quick, it's important.'

With a worried look at Gila, Bea reassured her, 'I'll be back in a moment, I promise.'

Several moments passed, before Leo remarked, 'So how shall we do this? Any suggestions?'

'*This?*' Gila quizzed, pretending not to understand. She refused to reveal her own discomfort. Not until she knew how he felt. Since yesterday morning when he'd shown concern when the baby surprised her by shifting during yoga, she'd become more unsure about things. All of which unfortunately centred around him. Probably an effect of being around each other again.

'Should I stand on one side of the garden and you on the other, while we carefully avoid coming into contact? Circulate with each of us heading in different directions? Perhaps we can time slot for when each of us buys a drink or grabs food from the buffet inside.'

'I'm sure we can be adult about this,' she said, not feeling a bit mature. All she did was remember every time she was in his company. Each one centred on a man who'd left her feeling unloved and unwanted. Where had this undiscovered sadistic streak come from?

'Of course,' Leo agreed. 'We share a home after all. Attending this party and being civil should be easy.'

'For seven days only,' she reminded him. Though now it was only six days and counting. 'Or until a hotel has a vacant room.'

He nodded and glanced down at the drink in his hand. 'I hadn't forgotten, Gila. Trust me, I haven't.'

Gila's gaze narrowed and she huffed under her breath. What exactly did he mean by that? Was he also counting the hours until she left?

Was he already regretting his offer for her to stay?

A commotion by the restaurant's patio doors caught her attention and halted her spiralling thoughts. Shifting to one side, she frowned when she spotted someone sprawled out on the ground.

'I think Nick's aunt Tom has fallen,' Leo murmured with concern. He placed his glass down on a nearby table.

Without exchanging another word, they hurried over to the woman and the small group already gathering around her. Their private dispute forgotten while someone hurt required their attention and help.

'Hey, Aunt Tom,' Leo greeted the old lady dressed in her usual navy jumper and skirt, spread-eagled on the patio. Looking like a small, dazed baby bird who'd just fallen out of a nest. 'Suffered a bit of a fall, I see?'

'Caught my foot on the chair and came down hard. Stupid new shoes, I knew I shouldn't have worn them. I never really got on with heels even as a young girl. You'd think I'd know better at eighty-five.'

Thomasina March, or Tom as everyone called her, flashed Leo and Gila a faint regal smile. 'How lovely to see you both again. Do be sweet and help me onto a chair, will you? These patio slabs are rather hard on one's bony posterior and the cold is starting to seep into my bones.'

Leo crouched and shook his head. 'Let's check you over first, shall we? Just in case you've broken something important. Now, does anything throb or hurt?'

'Mainly my pride, young Leo,' Tom answered with a resigned sigh. 'I haven't quite trumped the aging with dignity bit yet. I do try, but it's a struggle.'

'How about any bones?' Gila asked, squatting next to Leo. She instinctively rested a hand on his shoulder to help with her balance, glad she'd chosen to wear her jean dungarees and not a dress to the party. Less chance of dragging her hem along the ground or flashing her unattractive practical pregnancy underwear to innocent onlookers by mistake.

Aunt Tom snorted. 'I may be a clumsy old whatnot, but I'm pretty sure I mostly bumped, not snapped, when I hit the ground.'

'Best we check you for anything broken, though,' Leo said, trying not to laugh.

Aunt Tom stabbed a long bony finger into his arm. 'Young man, I've known you since you were a small boy. You will keep your hands to yourself. Instead, your darling wife may check my body for anything amiss or displaced.'

Unable to stop her own laughter, Gila gently pushed Leo to one side and slowly but carefully checked Aunt Tom's small frame for any serious damage or cuts. Finally, she gently prodded the lady's right arm, concerned by the sight of swelling around the delicate bony wrist.

'Does your wrist hurt, Aunt Tom?' Gila asked, glancing at the woman for an answer.

'Unfortunately it does appear to,' Aunt Tom replied. 'Classic thing of putting my hand out to stop myself when I fell, I'm afraid. It's a bit tender.'

Gila nodded and examined it once more. 'You've probably sprained it. Though I can't rule out that there might be a break with the way it's looking.'

Aunt Tom huffed. 'I'm such a silly old woman.'

'No, you're not,' Gila soothed. 'You tripped over, which can happen to any of us, but I think a trip to the hospital is best just to be certain. They'll also be able to give you something for the pain.'

'Oh, what a bother,' Aunt Tom complained. 'I'm sure it isn't broken. It just feels a bit achy and tender.'

'Best to be sure, though,' Leo agreed.

'I suppose, though I do hope not. I've the WI coach trip to Torquay next week. I can't miss it.'

Gila mollified her with a smile. 'I'm sure you'll be able to manage the trip with one arm working.'

'Even if it's a sprain, you'll need to rest the arm, though,' Leo added cautiously, his caring concern for the old woman apparent. 'Now Gila's given you the once-over, let's get you onto a chair, shall we?'

Nick and Leo gently and slowly lifted Aunt Tom off the patio slabs and settled her onto a nearby plastic chair. Softly squeezing the old lady's shoulder, Leo said, 'I'll go and fetch some ice for the wrist.'

Gila straightened and rechecked for any other signs of injury to the arm. Once she was sure there were no protruding bones or wounds, she helped Aunt Tom position the damaged limb across her body.

'I can see why you married him,' Aunt Tom said, her eyes following Leo as he walked away. 'Has a lovely manner. So caring. Always was a sweet child.'

Gila almost snorted. Caring? She'd once thought so too, but now she knew better. She sighed. 'He's a good doctor.'

'A good man, too,' Aunt Tom insisted. 'How much longer until baby arrives?'

Gila happily grabbed at the old lady's change of topic. With another smile, she replied, 'Just under four weeks.'

Aunt Tom raised her thin white eyebrows, her mouth puckering together in contemplation. 'So long? Are you sure? Don't be shocked if the baby isn't earlier. I inherited the gift from my grandmother. And she got it from her mother.'

'Gift?' Gila asked curiously.

'Of knowing when a baby is coming. I've never been wrong.'

Gila frowned, but dismissed the old lady's words. She knew her dates were right, thanks to her monthly cycle being regular. And first-time babies were commonly late in arriving.

'I always felt a little sorry for Leo, you know?' Aunt Tom said, changing the subject for the second time. Gila stiffened, not sure what to say. Surely Nick had informed his aunt that she and Leo had separated? He and Bea were the only friends who knew. Though the way the man was so happily in love with Bea, it might have slipped his mind.

'You did?'

'Yes, his childhood wasn't an easy one. Oh, his family were what many would call privileged, I suppose. Wealthy and liked people to know it. But from the age of twelve, when his sister arrived, he became a sort of surrogate parent. Leo's mother and father both worked very demanding, high-profile jobs in the city. Worked hours on end, often seven days a week. Left the children in the care of one nanny after another. Some well trained, others not so. Young women who grew to resent the long hours Leo's parents expected them to work. In the end they left it to Leo to bring Jodie up. A lot of responsibility for a young boy. Far too much. Social services should've stepped in, but his parents were well off and middle class, so of course no one questioned it at the time. No one looked beyond the respectable front door, I suppose. I wonder if anyone in our street even noticed.'

'*You* did,' Gila pointed out, reluctantly intrigued and concerned by the picture the old lady was providing of Leo's childhood. Although they'd discussed their pasts, Leo had always made his upbringing sound normal and similar to other people's. Yet, it seemed as though neglect and too much responsibility had filled his early years. Why hadn't he told her that?

'Nick tells me that his sister's death hit Leo hard. You know, I guess he must have felt as if he'd lost his own child in a way. The sibling he raised and loved. The guilt must have hurt worse though. As a doctor unable to help her fight her addiction. I understand his parents blame him. Still as self-centred as ever. Easier to blame someone else than admit your own failings. But the truth is his parents neglected both their children.'

Leo reappeared holding a red checked tea towel and carrying a plastic bucket of ice. 'Here, Tom, let's wrap this around your wrist. It will help with the swelling and numb some of the pain.'

Working together, Gila and Leo slipped the tea towel around Aunt Tom's arm and packed several ice cubes each side of her wrist to help ease the swelling. Once done, Leo gently returned the injured limb to its former position across her body. His movements slow and considerate. Never rushed or impatient. Just the way a good doctor treated his patients, but there was more to his actions. His genuine care and concern for the old lady was obvious and Gila could see how much he thought of Aunt Tom. But then patience was one of the things she always admired in Leo. He rarely became ruffled by events or situations. Always a clear practical mind when required. Her father had always lived by whatever twist or turn his emotions or moods took him, so Leo's cool level-headedness was always a comfort to her jaded soul.

'Keep your arm in this position to support it,' he advised with a smile.

Nick appeared once more at his side. 'Dad's going to run you to A & E for an X-ray, Aunt Tom.'

The old lady huffed, but allowed her brother and nephew to lead her from the garden and into a waiting car. With a quick thanks, she bid Leo and Gila goodbye.

Alone again, they watched the car drive away, before Gila turned to Leo. 'I think I'll head home. I'm afraid I'm not really in the mood for socialising. Hopefully Bea will be too distracted to notice my absence.'

Leo nodded, shoving his hands into his trouser pockets. 'I know what you mean. Do you mind if I come too?'

She hesitated for a second before answering, 'No, I don't mind, Leo.'

She smiled awkwardly, suddenly not sure how to act around him. Her conversation with Aunt Tom still lingering in her mind. Why did Leo's parents blame him for Jodie's death? Important information he'd never told her. Why not? Had he worried about her reaction, or, worse, felt he couldn't talk to her about it?

Was that why he'd shut her out those weeks before she'd left?

Not once had she ever considered that his perfect life might not have been what it appeared or thought to look beyond the fancy background to the real layers beneath Leo's family. On the few occasions she'd met his parents, she'd felt intimidated and inadequate. They'd never hidden their disappointment in their son's choice of wife and Gila's unforgivable lack of social connections.

But, thinking back, had she been so wrapped up in the negativity of her own past that she'd not contemplated Leo's early life might not be as flawless and perfect—well, apart from Jodie and her issues—as she thought? Leo had kept any time she'd spent with his parents brief and infrequent. Was that because he'd been concerned that she might find out the truth behind the swanky glint of his family's middle-class shine?

Perhaps it *was* time they talked. After all, how could she make a decision about her, Leo's and the baby's future when she suspected she didn't know everything from their past?

The narrowboat was delightfully peaceful after the noisy party. Gila kicked off her shoes and wriggled her toes, enjoying the freedom. Grabbing a ripe peach from a china bowl on the side, she padded into the lounge as Leo came from the opposite direction.

'I've started a bath for you. Your back's hurting, right?'

She nodded and smiled, refusing to be awkward or argumentative. Leo's ability to read her moods and body had always fascinated her. His knack of being able to tell when she required a hug, or to be left alone to brood, was surprisingly instinctive. No one in her life had ever bothered to read her that way. No one else had ever cared to.

'It's killing, to be honest. Pressing up against my spine must be baby's favourite position.'

'Go and grab a towel while I pour a glass of orange juice for you. You can sip it while you soak away the aches.'

She hesitated, then nodded, happy to do as he recommended. 'Thank you, Leo.'

He smiled softly before leaving to organise her drink.

Padding into the bedroom, Gila stripped out of her dungarees, top and underwear and wrapped a clean towel around her body. For the first time in months it felt nice to have someone fuss over her. Her father and Art had done their best over the years, but they were both old-school men who had struggled with the emotional needs of a young child. Leo, though, had always managed to make her feel secure. That was until Jodie's death, when he'd shut down and left her wondering what to do or how to help. She'd never faced a situation like it before and she'd panicked, convinced he was letting her go. Deserting her the way so many others had.

Heading for the minuscule bathroom, she found Leo waiting outside the room.

'Here's your drink,' he said, handing over a fresh glass of cold juice. His fingers bumped hers as she took the glass from him. Condensation ran down its sides and pooled against her sticky peach-juice fingertips. Running her tongue over her top lip, she hesitated, before asking, 'Leo, can we talk?'

Leo stared down at her for several seconds, before nodding, 'Okay. How about I sit out here while you bathe? If you leave the door open, we'll be able to hear each other. Is there something in particular you'd like to discuss?'

She moved towards the bathroom, but just before stepping inside, she glanced back over her shoulder. Not certain if it was a good idea or not, she said, 'This might seem odd, but will you tell me about your childhood?'

* * *

Leo slipped to the floor and rested his head against the plasterboard wall separating them. He'd expected Gila to ask something mundane or general, but her question about his childhood threw him. What caused her to want to delve into a time in his life he rarely considered or discussed these days? He almost wished she'd asked anything but that.

He closed his eyes and the smell of roses and cucumber drifted through the half-open door. The aroma courtesy of the bar of soap Gila always bought from a local health shop. She rarely wore perfume, preferring a simpler, cleaner scent. Something that didn't overpower the senses. It reminded him of long-ago nights in bed, snuggled together. The two of them wrapped completely and wholly into each other. Skin touching skin, their heartbeats twinned in a matching rhythm.

He'd give anything to enter the bathroom and kiss her. To sink into her body and return to the special place where he was simply Leo. Not the husband, brother, son or doctor. But just Leo, the man.

'Leo?'

He heard her gentle prompting for him to start. Not wanting to disappoint Gila now she was finally talking to him without looking as though she wanted to grind him into the ground, he faltered for a moment, uncertain how to begin.

'I'm not sure where to start,' he admitted. 'You know most everything about my childhood. My parents were two very successful city—'

'No, not the boring stuff,' she interrupted. 'But your day-to-day life. Nick's aunt mentioned your parents employed nannies. You never told me that.'

Her sudden interest in his past started to make sense. Obviously, Aunt Tom had said something to Gila when he'd left them alone while he'd fetched the ice and towel. He wasn't sure he liked the idea of them discussing his family. He'd made a point to keep Gila away from his parents, knowing what hard work they were to be around and their prickly attitude towards her because of their own prejudices. They viewed his and Gila's marriage as a temporary inconvenience. His father had even given Leo the number of a solicitor who specialised in divorce the morning of their wedding. A number Leo had immediately thrown away. So what had the old lady said to raise Gila's curiosity?

'Yeah, a lot of nannies, until the agencies stopped sending them amid complaints of exploitation. My parents took advantage of their employees. After all, why care for your own children when there's more interesting and entertaining events like meetings or parties to attend?'

'But it's what parents do,' she argued. 'They look after their babies.'

He chuckled dryly. 'You know yourself that parents come in all guises. Some adequate, some less so.'

'And yours?' Gila probed.

'Absent mostly,' he said with a heavy sigh. 'They never considered their children as a barrier to living the life they really wanted. We were not a responsibility, they believed, who had the right to disrupt the freedom of their social lives. Jodie and I were just two events they ticked off a pre-prepared life list. Their friends had children, so of course they had to produce some, too. Only they preferred the type of offspring who stayed behind a nursery door and never cluttered the house with their barely tolerated presence or belongings.'

'But that's terrible,' Gila said, disapproval lacing her voice.

'It's what it was,' Leo murmured. 'We move on, don't we? Make sure we do things differently in our own lives, with our own children. Never repeat our parents' mistakes and faults.'

'Yes, I suppose. But…'

'What?' he coaxed, hearing concern in her tone. Did hearing about his upbringing cause her to worry over whether he was capable of being a good parent to his own child? He'd already botched up being a husband and brother, hadn't he? Was she now doubting his ability in the role of a father? Was there any way he could prove he'd never be like his own parents when he'd already bombed so badly in other relationships?

'*We* both have busy careers…' she pointed out.

So it wasn't just him she was concerned for, it was both of them. 'I'll give up my career if our child needs more. I'll never put my job before our son or daughter.'

'I won't either,' she promised solemnly. 'Oh, Leo, what happened to us?'

Leo closed his eyes and breathed slowly. The one question he had asked himself so many times. Finally, he acknowledged, 'I shut you out, Gila. After my sister's death. I'm sorry, I did that.'

'Did I do something to make you?' she asked. 'Did I not support you? Not show you how much I cared?'

Fresh pain shot through him at her soft anxious queries. The slight tremble in her voice shaming him. Breaking him apart a little bit more. 'I swear you did nothing wrong, Gila. It was all me. Not you.'

'I didn't help you much, though, did I?' she said. 'When Jodie died, I mean. I wasn't any real comfort to you other than staying with you in her hospital room. In nursing college they teach you how to be kind and supportive to patients and their family members. But it's easy to be that way with a stranger, because it doesn't truly affect you, does it? Things may upset or sadden you at work, but the training helps you to deal with it. To put it in a place where your raw emotions are protected and you can keep some perspective. You have to otherwise you wouldn't be able to do the job, or at least not for long. But I didn't know what to do when confronted with your pain. I had no idea how to reach out or help you. I tried, but you refused to let me in.'

Horrified by the way she was blaming herself, Leo searched for the right words to explain. To find a cohesive way to describe that period in a way that would make sense to Gila and stop any ill-founded guilt she might carry. 'I believe Jodie never wanted to stop being an addict, or for the pain of losing Russ to leave. It was the only connection she had with him. The truth is the Jodie I knew died the day Russ did. The woman she became was nothing but a stranger I was related to.'

'I always felt she resented me in your life,' Gila admitted quietly. Revealing a feeling she'd always kept to herself, not wanting to upset him. 'Especially in the beginning when she made it clear she didn't like me.'

Leo nodded even though Gila couldn't see him, recalling the arguments his sister had caused between them. The way she'd ignored Gila whenever they'd met. Or the lies she would tell when Leo left the room. Lies created in the hope that Gila would believe them and leave Leo. So Jodie could once again have him all to herself.

'I think she was jealous at times. I had a career, a home and you. She in turn had drugs and sad, old memories. She'd never really shared me with anyone else. She grew up with me on one side and Russ on the other. Always there to support her when she found things tough and struggled. Then Russ died and everything she viewed as safe suddenly ended.'

The sound of trickling water drifted from the bathroom. Leo imagined Gila shifting in the warm bath, conjuring images of it running over her sleek, pale flesh as she moved around the bathtub.

A noise brought his head up and he found she now stood beside him, wrapped in a pink towel. Her cheeks rosy from the bath and tiny tendrils of her damp hair curled against her neck. His fingers itched to play with the curls, but he didn't dare.

Crouching, she said, 'I'm sorry about Jodie, Leo. I really am.'

He nodded, squeezing his hands into fists to stop them from reaching out and sliding over the curve of her shoulder. His fingers tingled with the need to brush away the drops of bath water scattering the skin around her collarbone. Every part of him yearned to lean forward and kiss her soft mouth and make the pain and the hurt of the last few months melt away for just a few seconds. 'Me, too.'

'It's all such a mess, isn't it?' she whispered.

He nodded and glanced at her bump covered by just the towel. 'Yeah, but we have the baby to look forward to. I swear I'll do a better job as a father than I have as a husband.'

She tensed slightly and then nodded. 'Let's just take it slowly. Yes?'

Leo nodded, grateful for the chance she was offering.

Gila reached out and grabbed his fist, uncurling it. She placed it flat against her stomach, keeping her eyes lowered as though fearing he might pull away. 'Would you like to feel the baby move and kick?'

Leo swallowed, his eyes stinging, and whispered back, 'Yes, Gila. I'd love to.'

She looked up then and met his gaze. Her grey eyes holding his own. 'There...can you feel that?'

Leo grinned and a single tear rolled from the corner of his eye as a firm thud vibrated through the towel and hit him in the centre of his palm. His unborn child's kick. The baby he'd helped to create. 'Yes, sweetheart. I can.'

CHAPTER SEVEN

GILA LIFTED THE small glass dome-shaped cloche and watered the barely sprouting onion seed inside the black plastic pot. Replacing the cloche back over the container, she slowly moved on to the next veg box, this time mini beetroot, and also gave it a decent drenching of water from the pink watering can.

She'd come out onto the narrowboat's roof garden to think and the slowly encompassing darkness as the late afternoon eased into early evening created the perfect place to mull over her troubled and confused thoughts.

What was she supposed to do about Leo? Everything she'd thought over the last few months suddenly felt irrelevant now she'd discarded her own hurt feelings to one side and observed the situation from his point of view. Had she really not done that before? Not even once? The awful truth was, she hadn't. Not really.

She watered another box of barely grown vegetables and sighed at her own self-centred behaviour. When had she become so uncaring? Surely it wasn't her true nature to see everything from only her own aspect and disregard other people's? But thinking back to after Jodie's death and the following horrible weeks when Leo slowly circled away from her, emotionally pushing her aside with his continued silence and indifference, she couldn't recall one moment when she'd stopped and fully reflected on his feelings, or pondered on how deeply his grief truly went. Oh, she wasn't completely insensitive and cold-hearted. She'd known he was upset and miserable, but she'd never questioned that there could be more behind the expected stress and emotions that everyone suffered when going through the initial stages of mourning. Not once had she suspected his grieving might also be mixed with guilt because he'd virtually raised his sister from birth and then found himself unable to help her in the end.

But then how could she have known when he'd never told her? Not once had he revealed the truth concerning his and his sister's early relationship, or how he'd taken on the role of parent. And how could Gila have helped him when Leo had never reached out to her? Never made that initial move or effort to communicate the pain inside him. Pain he had to endure and come through if they were ever going to move forward.

Gila thought back to the hours she and Leo had sat in Jodie's hospital room. She'd thought it strange that his parents hadn't travelled over from Spain, and now she knew the reason why. They were indifferent to their own daughter's welfare, and also too selfish to concern themselves with the pain Leo was going through.

And her? Wasn't marriage supposed to be a partnership where each person committed to the other through good and bad? Had she only played at the good and when the bad had come hurling along to test her, she'd failed dismally? Hadn't she in fact without meaning to, like Leo's parents, neglected him? The man she had sworn to love and help. The male who'd been her world.

So was the truth not whether he had abandoned *her*, but that *she* had actually abandoned him, too? Somehow, they had both lost one another and their closeness due to their inability to talk honestly to each other?

Gila sighed, shaking her head. Her thoughts leaving her more confused than ever. Which one of them was guilty of letting the other down? For the first time in months, she wasn't so sure of the answer.

Placing the empty watering can down beside the box, careful not to catch either the hem of her nightdress or dressing gown on the dripping plastic rose, she rested her hands on her hips and stared along the canal's length.

Several ducks swam past, sending a quack of hello in her direction. A robin flew out from a tree to land on a narrowboat further along, much to the surprise of the passengers sitting on the roof enjoying an evening cocktail. Gila chuckled and turned away, before resuming her silent wonderings.

Was she culpable of failing to see and put Leo's heartache before her own wounded feelings? Allowing him to disappear alone into his sorrow because she hadn't known how to deal with it or him? Giving into the old habit of running away rather than stay and face a situation she had no idea how to react to?

A thread of guilt-ridden shame twisted through her, prodding at her conscience. Well, she hadn't provided much help during that time, had she?

She reflected back on their courtship. That period of their relationship had been both quick and intense. Both had been eager to spend what little free time they had with each other. Each purposely giving only sketchy accounts of their family backgrounds when questioned. Was it because they were equally ashamed of their childhoods and hoped neither ever discovered that they were less than the person they liked to portray to the world? That semi-perfect character an individual showed when desperate to hide their imperfections, but keen to impress someone new into liking them.

Was that yet another mistake they'd made in their relationship? Had they never revealed their true selves to the other? Never taken the time to really discover the people deep inside their hearts? She didn't have an answer to any of her ponderings, but what she *did* understand was that her husband's relationship with his sister had been more complex than just siblings. Was Aunt Tom correct when she stated that Leo must have felt as though he'd failed as both a doctor and a brother when Jodie died?

When Gila and Leo first started dating, she'd tried to reach out to Jodie, wanting to help the younger woman with her problems. But Jodie had quickly made it clear that she'd neither sought Gila's help nor liked her existence in her brother's life. Initially, not upset by Jodie's resistance, Gila had waited several weeks before trying again. Keen to help both Leo and his sister in any way she could, eager to become the girl's friend, but Jodie had resented and blocked every attempt and eventually accused Gila of harassing her.

And then the lies had begun. At first silly things like saying Gila had made nasty comments when Leo was out of the room. Then she'd call Gila's mobile at night when Leo was working a shift and say she'd seen him with another woman. Trying to worm doubt and suspicion into their relationship whenever she could.

Unsure how to handle the situation, and not about to believe anything Jodie said, Gila had stepped back when Leo had suggested she wait until Jodie had a chance to get to know her better. The excuses Leo had made for his sister's behaviour had sometimes been frustrating, but she'd trusted that he understood Jodie best and that things would eventually improve. Unfortunately the opportunity to get closer had never materialised because the other woman had suddenly insisted on meeting Leo alone and often away from the narrowboat.

And truthfully, Gila had felt relieved not to

have to deal with Jodie's spiteful and childish behaviour any more. As much as she'd wished to help her, Gila had never expected when she married Leo to have the shadow of Jodie's dislike, resentment and addiction hovering over them.

But how painful for Leo to lose his sister. Not having grown up with siblings, Gila struggled to grasp or appreciate how such a connection worked between people. Those close complexities that only brothers and sisters understood. But she did know Leo was not a man who walked away from his responsibilities easily. Even when *they'd* split up, he'd still made certain she was cared for financially by depositing money into her bank account every month. She hadn't asked him to and had even demanded he stop, but every month the money arrived for her to use.

Folding her arms, Gila glanced at the darkening sky, taking in the way the clouds sat in a mass of small puffy balls above her. Though singular in shape they were all connected to each other, unlike her and Leo.

When Leo's sister had passed away, instead of clinging to one another the way the clouds overhead did, they'd slowly and painfully glided apart.

Was she a terrible person to put her feelings before the person she loved? Wasn't that a big no-no rule when in a committed relationship? To be honest, she didn't know. Leo was the only man she'd ever fallen in love with. The one male she'd allowed herself to trust completely. The whole romance game totally unfamiliar and confusing to her. An emotional and sexual maze of wrong turns and dos and don'ts. Most of which she didn't understand. But she did recall reading a book years before, one she'd borrowed from a library, which stated certain important rules in love. Had putting your partner's needs first been one of them?

Perhaps she wasn't cut out for love? Maybe seeing and living through her father's many failed attempts had crushed all emotion and compassion inside her? Was she as flawed in the love game as he'd been? Chasing after some fantasy sentiment that in truth didn't exist. Just as incapable of experiencing it for longer than a few weeks, several months or at the most a year.

A sound from the other end of the narrowboat attracted her attention and she glanced up to see Leo climbing the steps to the roof. He paused, his hands gripping the metal rails on each side. Rails he'd fixed there when they'd first learnt she was expecting the baby, after declaring he didn't want to risk her falling or hurting herself whenever she went onto the roof.

Her heartbeat increased as she stood silently taking him in. Why did the sight of him still ignite such a warm sensation deep inside her? Surely her body should know not to skip or respond every time he came into her vicinity? When would her fingers stop wanting to brush his thick dark fringe from his face, or her disloyal lips lose the urge to kiss his?

Gila forced a smile as he stepped onto the roof and walked towards her. His easy, long strides so memorable and comforting. She loved the way he walked. It caused her to think of hazy summer afternoons and warm smooth brandy with just a hint of walnut and black pepper. Earthy tastes with a kick of heat.

'How's the gardening going?' he asked, glancing to where the watering can dripped a small puddle.

'Want one?' she asked, pulling a cherry from her dressing-gown pocket. She'd grabbed a handful before leaving the kitchen, figuring it was better to eat these than the cream cake she really craved.

Leo nodded and reached for the offered

fruit. Taking it, he popped it into his mouth and murmured, 'Hmm, nice.'

She agreed, her traitorous eyes watching his mouth as he chewed the cherry. How her tongue yearned to lick the corner, just by the faint small scar he'd received a couple of years before after attempting extreme cross-country running for the first time and colliding with a tree halfway round the course.

But that would be a mistake and she'd already made plenty. Ones she'd learnt to regret. At this moment, she didn't know what to think. She just knew that the past wasn't as simple as she'd thought.

'I'm amazed the plants are so healthy—' She suddenly broke off. Out here in the semi-darkness with the peace interrupted only by the sound of classical music and laughter drifting from a couple of the nearby houses, it seemed wrong to drag up all the unpleasantness between them. Not when they'd achieved some kind of unspoken truce for the evening.

'I've tried my best to keep the garden going for you,' Leo murmured, obviously guessing her unspoken words. He shifted closer but didn't touch her.

She glanced around at the plastic boxes filled with winter vegetables and the young tender shoots of spring and summer ones.

Plants she'd sown and tended before she left, not thinking she wouldn't be around to maintain or harvest them. Yet the plants were healthy and happy because Leo had taken the trouble to care and water them. Why? The garden had always been her interest and hobby. Was it really as he said and he'd done it for her? Had he wanted to show that he cared enough to keep her small winter garden going?

She hadn't bothered to grow anything on her uncle's narrowboat. Her enthusiasm for everything had waned during the long weeks living there. But Leo had fussed and cared for this mini garden, never knowing whether his efforts would be wasted or not. It touched her heart that he'd done so.

'Want another?' she asked, pulling a second dark shiny cherry from her pocket. Unsure whether to thank him or demand answers. Tonight they'd talked but so many questions still plagued her mind.

Leo chuckled and accepted it. Glancing around the surroundings, he said, 'It's so calm out here, isn't it?'

Gila gazed at him, taking in the long line of his neck and the way his hair curled against the loose collar of his T-shirt. He appeared relaxed and content. Happy in himself. Was it how he felt inside, though? Or did deeper emotions bubble beneath the skin in readiness to spill out?

'Unlike life,' she murmured.

He nodded and turned her way. 'It's certainly not been quiet and uneventful recently, has it? For either of us.'

A hard kick from the baby prevented her from replying. Gila laughed and placed a hand to her stomach. 'I think little one has woken up again.'

'Do you have everything you need for the baby?' Leo asked, shifting the focus from the past and to the future. 'Is there anything I can help with?'

She rubbed a loving hand over their child. 'There's a few things I need to pick up. Last-minute stuff, you know? Items I've hesitated to buy in case I jinxed things. Silly superstitious nonsense, really.'

'I don't think it's silly. Are you excited?' he asked.

'Yes,' she admitted. 'And a little scared, too. I mean, of course I've studied the subject for years and helped countless women through their births, but it's still the first time for me. I'm going to find out how it really feels to give birth to a baby, instead of reading and learning by observing others. How about you? Are *you* excited?'

He hesitated for a second before solemnly declaring, 'I can't wait to be a daddy.'

She licked her lower lip. 'I suppose we should think about what's going to happen after the baby's here. How we co-parent.'

He touched her other hand, his fingers loosely linking with her own. 'There's plenty of time for those decisions.'

She frowned, her brain silently shouting to pull her hand away, but her body hesitated. 'Is there? The weeks are whizzing past.'

His fingers squeezed hers lightly. 'Look, Gila, there's something I want to tell you.'

A cold trickle travelled slowly along her spine, her brain yelling at her to be wary because when a person said those words it rarely brought joy to the receiver. Was this when he admitted he wanted a divorce? That he no longer saw a future together for them? This sweet moment ruined by the intrusion of ugly realism.

'There's no rush,' she began.

'No, it's important you hear this,' he interrupted her, his tone firm and determined. Making it clear he wasn't going to be put off by any attempt she made to redirect the conversation. The expression on his face reminded her of the times when her father would inform her that, yet again, they were going to live with another woman or move to a different country.

She glanced away, her eyes falling on a passing insect. How she'd love to swap bodies with that creature and scuttle away into a small hole or deep crevice. Or jump overboard into the water and swim somewhere new. But she'd tried to do that when she left months before and she'd discovered life refused to be so easily avoided, so instead she nodded. 'Okay, tell me what you wish to say.'

'The thing is, I've been seeing—'

She yanked her hand from his, not intending to hear any more. Resisting the impulse to cover her ears and sing loudly like a hysterical child, she snapped, 'Don't, Leo. Please, don't. I can guess what you are about to say and I don't want to know. Not tonight.'

Not when she was just accepting that the faults in their marriage might not all be his.

Leo grasped her arm to prevent her from moving away. His hold firm but not painful. 'Gila, what is it you think I'm going to say?'

She sucked in a deep breath and tried to bury the fear that had plagued her most of her life. How many more times would a male insist on influencing the course of her life without regard for her feelings, just so they could have everything their own way? How many times had her own father put a woman he hardly knew before *her* safety and welfare? His own child's needs irrelevant when matched against his own. Did Leo now intend to add yet another fracture to her already sore and shattered heart? Did he plan to show her yet again how unimportant she was?

'If you want a divorce, then I'd prefer you didn't tell me until after the baby is born. Let me have time to concentrate on our child and forget everything else for a while. *Please*, Leo.'

Leo was stunned at her words. A divorce? Was she kidding? Did she really think he was going to tell her such rubbish only weeks from their child's birth?

God, did she not realise how utterly in love with her he was? How he didn't see other women because she'd ruined him for anyone but her? No one smiled the way she did, nor caused his heart to flip, or even roused his temper the way only she could. For him there was no one else, but obviously she no longer trusted what he said. All his fault and his problem to mend.

Tonight he'd waited before searching Gila

out. His concentration refusing to settle on the work papers he'd tried to bury himself in after their earlier conversation. The memory of his palm placed over their growing child, and the delightful shock when the baby kicked, one he would always treasure.

But a feeling of unfinished business remained since they'd parted. A strong sense that there was so much more to share. Now he'd finally started to open up to Gila and admit the secrets in his heart, he yearned to get it all out. To tell her everything and let her hear exactly what he'd tried to protect her from and why. Why now when he couldn't before, he didn't know, but it just felt time to at least try.

How could they find a pathway towards any honest future, no matter how they raised their child, if the prior secrets still clung and stuck to him with the same tenacity of a rampant vine intent on smothering everything? Wasn't it crucial to expose and deal with the past for good if they hoped to rebuild?

Deciding to get the conversation started, because circling around sent them in the wrong direction and hurt Gila unnecessarily, Leo gathered his courage. He saw the clear desire to run in his wife's guarded wary gaze, but gently drew her towards him, until her body stopped next to his. The curve of her stomach nestling against his flat one. Cupping her cheek, he whispered, 'You think I want a divorce?'

'Don't you?' she stammered. 'Don't you want to finish everything with me and start again?'

'No, my darling. Besides we'll never be finished when we share a child.'

Or while every part of my heart still belongs to you.

He shook his head and insisted, 'I don't want a divorce. Why would you think I would?'

She shrugged and flushed. 'I don't know. I suppose it came into my head when you said you wanted to talk. I thought that maybe you'd met someone.'

'Well, please allow that thought to leave because there's no one else I'm interested in and any decision we make about divorcing can wait.'

'Good,' she said shakily.

Leo smiled and probed, 'Good?'

She stiffened and glanced away. 'Well, yes. Separation can be hard without other people becoming involved and confusing things. Or so others say.'

His thumb gently caressed the corner of her

mouth. 'I get that you're not ready to hear that you're the only one I want because I've hurt you. That's my sorrow to carry and I always will. But what I want to share with you is this. I *have* actually been seeing someone, but it isn't for any romantic reasons or intentions. It's simply to do with my mental well-being.'

She frowned and met his gaze. Her grey eyes searching his face for clues to what he meant. 'I don't understand.'

He sensed her tension and confusion. Not wanting to prolong the moment now he'd started, Leo continued, 'For the last few months I've had weekly sessions with a grief counsellor. Basically, since you walked out on me.'

She stared at him trying to make logic of his words. Opening her mouth, she shut it again, before finally asking, 'A counsellor? You?'

He nodded, feeling a self-conscious flush warm his skin. He didn't know why he felt so awkward talking about this, he certainly wasn't ashamed of seeking help. But this was the woman he'd always longed to astonish and amaze. The female he'd wanted to be a hero to. 'Yes.'

'But why?'

'Because when you left, I finally admitted

to myself the mess I was in, and I understood that if I ever hoped to right things between us, I needed to make sense of the anguish consuming me.'

'Oh, Leo,' she said, placing her hand over his where it still rested against her face. 'I thought… I…didn't…'

'What?'

'It doesn't matter. I suppose I never thought you would visit a counsellor.'

He let out a sharp noise that was neither a laugh nor a groan. But definitely a sound of discomfort. 'Why—because I'm a doctor? A man?'

'No,' she said. 'Because you constantly refused to talk to me.'

'Only because I wasn't sure what to tell you,' he confessed. 'Truth is, I'm exactly the person who needed to find help and I'm not too proud to say so. But before you left, I couldn't see it.'

Gila stared at him. 'We've created such a muddle of everything, haven't we?'

'But we're trying to mend it, aren't we?' His gaze held hers, his question hanging between them. What if Gila viewed his reaching out to a professional as a weakness? What if she concluded that she didn't want him any more because of it? Now she knew about the counselling sessions would she see him as broken and flawed? Less of a person? A sad image of a man? Resent him for talking to a stranger when he'd stubbornly shied away from opening up to her?

'Isn't that all that matters?' he asked, concerned when Gila stayed silent. 'That we at least try to make amends for the confusion of the past.'

CHAPTER EIGHT

GILA STEPPED OFF the bus and stared at the large post-war concrete hospital situated across the street. People streamed in and out of the main entrance, dotted by the odd white-coated medic. A couple of paramedics, distinctive in their green uniforms, wheeled a patient stretched out on a trolley from the back of an ambulance, closely followed inside by a trio of chatting nurses, possibly returning from their lunch break.

Gila breathed in a deep, fortifying breath and then crossed the road and walked towards the building, heading for the hospital's main section, where Leo worked his morning shift.

She'd travelled to the hospital on a whim and now she desperately prayed she wasn't making a mistake. During the bus journey into the city, she'd silently debated with herself, unsure whether her trip would end with a positive result or a negative one. But after last night, when Leo had stated his eagerness over the baby's arrival, she'd woken up this morning with the idea that he might like to join her on her shopping trip to buy the last few things she needed before their baby's birth.

Heading along the wide and long hospital corridors in the direction of the A & E department, Gila passed streams of hurrying people, many with tight, worried faces as they headed to appointments or visited sick friends and family. Each in a bubble of their own thoughts and fears.

Reaching A & E, she took in the full and busy seating area, before making her way over to a harassed-looking middle-aged nurse sitting behind the main desk, glaring at a computer screen.

'Hi, can I help you?' the nurse asked with a distracted, weary smile. She took in Gila's pregnancy bump, and immediately declared, 'If you're searching for the maternity unit, I'm afraid you've taken a wrong turn. We're Accident and Emergency. So unless you've broken, burnt or cut something or worse, then you're in the wrong place.'

Gila shook her head and rested a hand on the desk. 'Actually, I'd like to speak to Dr Wright.'

The nurse shot her a surprised look before

glancing around. 'He should be here some-where. I think he's recently finished with a patient. As you can see, we're really busy today. Are you a patient's relative? Only he won't be able to talk to you about them if you are.'

'No, I'm not,' Gila replied, before the woman could come up with any other reason to shoo her from the department. She hesitated, not sure whether to admit her marital connection to Leo or not. Did she still maintain the right to call herself his spouse when they were no lon-ger romantically involved? Though last night he'd insisted he wanted to sort things between them, what did he mean by that? Did he want their lives to go back to how they were or cre-ate a new link? Did he see their future sepa-rate, but joined by their child, or as a couple living together? Was it even possible to do so after the hurt and misunderstanding they'd experienced? And say they tried again, what would happen next time a problem or dilemma blotted their lives? Because she never wanted to experience the same sickening feeling of dismissal and abandonment from him again. She'd faced many tough hardships in her child-hood, but to lose Leo twice would destroy her.

'Gila?'

She sagged with relief when a familiar

male voice prevented her from having to explain further to the woman behind the desk. Turning, she came face to face with the man she'd come to speak with. Wearing his doctor's coat over blue scrubs, Leo resembled every bit the medic he was. Tall, capable and distractingly handsome.

He moved closer, touching her elbow. His hold gentle through the thick layer of her coat. A concerned frown creased his brow. 'Is everything okay? The baby?'

She nodded, instantly wanting to ease his worry and concern. 'We're both fine. I just wanted…' Her words trailed off as she realised the nurse behind the desk was blatantly listening to their conversation. 'Can we talk somewhere private for a moment?'

'Of course,' he said, glaring at the nurse. 'Excuse us, I need to speak to my wife for a few moments.'

'Wife?' the woman repeated, but Leo didn't wait around to confirm, intent only on gently directing Gila over to a quiet corner in the room, close to a large window overlooking a small garden. Several patients were sitting on benches, enjoying the peaceful surroundings.

'The reason I'm here is to…' Gila stopped, suddenly unsure whether this was a good idea. A wave of self-consciousness consumed her. How to explain her reason for asking without making herself sound desperate for his company? Because she really wasn't. She just thought he might like to help choose the last few items. She was doing her part to be nice and accommodating. All she needed to do was make it sound as though she wasn't the least bit bothered either way by his answer. If he declined the invitation or had other plans, then she'd just leave and do the shopping on her own. No big deal. Nothing to get worked up over. Just ask the question and leave the rest to him.

'The reason I'm here is…' she began again.

And stopped for the second time and contemplated him. What if he didn't want to come with her? What if he thought it best to go back to scarcely communicating? He'd said he still wanted her, but in what way? After the last couple of days, when they'd begun to share how they felt, a part of her secretly hoped to find some new balance in their relationship. Urgh, she was starting to get a headache from all the indecision.

'Gila? What is it?' Leo asked, gently nudging her arm.

Shaking away the doubts, she accepted it was too late to change her mind. 'I'm going shopping for a pram. I haven't organised one

yet, you see. And time is running out and—
I've put it off, to be honest—bad luck and
all that business new mothers-in-waiting are
warned against and I thought maybe you
would like to—'

'I'd love to come with you,' Leo smoothly
butted in. A twinkle of pleasure glimmering
in his eyes. 'When do you wish to go?'

'Today,' she said, ignoring the burst of happiness his acceptance caused to bloom. How
ridiculous to be so pleased by his agreement
to join her in a task tons of people performed
every day. Yet, she was. Why it meant so
much to her she'd mull over later, but now she
just wanted to leave the hospital and head to
the shops before Leo changed his mind or an
incoming emergency prevented him.

Leo checked his watch. 'I finish my shift
in ten minutes. Why don't you wait here for
me?'

She nodded, resisting the urge to clap her
hands in excitement. They were going to pick
out a pram, for their baby, together. For the
first time in weeks exhilaration fizzed like
sparkling giddy bubbles inside her. 'Sounds
great.'

Leo nodded before turning away. Suddenly
he stopped and spun back. Shooting her a
grin, he said, 'Thank you, Gila.'

Confused and slightly dazed from his smile, she stammered, 'What for?'

'For including me,' he said simply, before walking off.

'This pram is so cute,' Leo declared, rolling the pink pram back and forth across the shop floor. His large hand out of place on the immaculate rubber handles. Very soon that same hand would hold their child. Enfold its small, delicate body in his strong grasp. Cradle their son or daughter in the protection of love. The thought sent goosebumps scattering over Gila's skin.

'Not so cute if the baby is male, though,' Gila mused, taking Leo's elbow and manoeuvring him over to a row of neutral-colour prams and pushchairs neatly displayed on the other side of the baby department in the well-known London store. 'We need a pram which is both colour neutral and also converts into a pushchair as the baby grows and their requirements change.'

'So no pink or blue,' Leo said. 'Unless you know what sex the baby is?'

'I don't, and definitely not,' she agreed, turning her attention back to the prams in front of them.

The sound of laughter and cooing coming

from a couple standing a few feet away drew Gila's attention. The way the pair tenderly smiled to each other while searching through a rail of brightly coloured baby clothes made her heart twinge. Wasn't that how parents-to-be were supposed to behave when buying for a new baby? All joyful and happy. Perhaps she and Leo would have participated in similar tender moments if she'd stayed a little longer and seen the depth of his sadness. If only he'd talked to her when she'd asked him to.

But they hadn't done either. Instead she had deserted him, wrapped up and troubled with her own dissatisfaction and bewilderment. Concerned mainly with making her husband see the damage to their marriage his rejection was causing.

She glanced away, her gaze falling on a black pram with soft grey lining close to where she stood. Stylish in its simplicity, it drew her. The colours suitable for either a girl or boy. Neutral but not bland and boring. Tasteful and not garish and patterned like some of the other prams. Walking over to it, Gila hesitantly placed her hand on the handle and gave it a small push, instinctively knowing that this pram was the one for them as it smoothly rolled back and forth on the tiled floor.

'This one's nice,' she murmured.

Leo joined her, placing his hand next to hers. Gila resisted the urge to release her hold on the handle, and instead took in the physical differences between their hands. Hers, pale and slim, Leo's long, dark and strong. Heat radiated from his skin, mutely enticing her to touch him. To feel the comforting heat from his body.

'What do you think?' she asked, shifting her hand away. If she left it there any longer, she'd give into the temptation to stretch out her little finger and touch his thumb. To connect with him in some small way.

'You're right,' Leo said. 'It's lovely. Perfect, in fact. Do you like it enough to buy it?'

She nodded, already visualising their child laid out inside it. Dressed in a cute all-in-one, kicking its little legs in the air. A flutter of longing tumbled through her and she touched her stomach. Soon she would be able to hold her baby. See its sweet little face. Soon they would both meet their child. And what kind of relationship would they be bringing their innocent son or daughter into? Where its parents lived separately? Where they behaved like polite strangers towards one another, both wary of upsetting the delicate equilibrium between them?

Pushing her silent contemplations to one side, she answered his question. 'Yes, I do.'

'And it converts into a pushchair?' Leo checked, glancing at the large information label hanging from the handle. A minute later, he grinned and nodded. 'It says it does.'

'Good,' Gila said, relieved it suited all their needs.

'Then this is the pram for us,' Leo agreed, giving the handle a final fond pat. 'Let's go and ask someone about it, shall we?'

Gila hesitated, then reached out to stop him from moving away. 'But do *you* like it, Leo?'

'Does it matter?' he asked, giving her a questioning glance.

Stunned by his question, she paused. Was that what he thought? That his opinion didn't matter? Was that why he'd never reached out to her when he required help? Did he believe his wants and needs were less relevant or important? That she wasn't interested in his wishes?

It wasn't true. She wanted to know exactly how he felt or what he thought. She always had. She hated the idea that he might be holding back from airing either. Shouldn't sharing their views and beliefs with each other be easy and natural?

'Of course,' she replied. 'The decision over which pram should be both of ours.'

Leo gave the pram another once-over, then shoved his hands into his trouser pockets. After a second, he asked, 'What's this really about, Gila?'

'The pram,' she said, but he stopped her with a shake of his head.

'No, why are you really asking if I like it? It's more than this being a joint choice, isn't it? What's truly bothering you? Have I said something to upset you?'

She shrugged, irritated by his accurate observation. Of course, he would search beyond a simple question for deeper information. His mind trained to view every topic from all angles and levels. 'I just don't want you to think I don't care about your opinion, that's all. Thinking back over our marriage I realise I may not always have considered your view on things, and I don't want you to feel that I don't respect or value it.'

Leo listened, then placed an arm across her shoulders and drew her close. Bending his head, he whispered, 'I've never felt you didn't care, Gila. Not once.'

Glancing up, she ignored the tickling warmth of his breath against her skin. She refused to be diverted by physical distractions when his comments were too important. Or rather he was too important. 'Honestly?'

He nodded and repeated, 'Not once.'

'But when I left—' She frowned, not finishing the sentence. How could he not feel some sense of resentment?

He held her tighter and continued, 'You left because you *did* care. I've always known that.'

Relieved, she said, 'Good.'

He pulled her closer for a second before easing back slightly.

'So can we go and buy the pram now?' he asked, sending her an indulgent smile. His arm still lingered casually on her shoulders. Its hold comforting and informal.

'Yes, I think we should. There's still a few other things we need to pick up, though.'

'Good,' Leo said, dropping his arm to grasp her hand. Silently, he led the way towards the counter, where a smartly dressed staff member stood speaking with a younger woman similarly dressed, but who sat on a chair. The younger female appeared to be having difficulty speaking and kept shaking her head at the other woman's questions.

With a heavy sigh, the older woman turned to Leo and Gila and forced a polite smile in their direction. 'Hello, can I be of assistance?'

'Hi, we'd like to buy one of your prams. The black and grey one that converts into—' Leo broke off as Gila tugged on his sleeve. Glancing down, he asked, 'Is something wrong?'

Gila nodded towards the shop assistant sitting on the chair. 'I think someone else might need our help first. She seems to be struggling to breathe correctly.'

Leo shifted his attention to the young female, before flicking his gaze to her colleague. 'Excuse me, but is your friend all right? She seems to be in some physical distress.'

'She's new. Started today, but she is feeling a little unwell,' the woman said, glancing worriedly at the younger woman. 'I've suggested she go to the staffroom and grab a drink of water but she refuses to listen and insisted on staying in case we become busy.'

Gila rounded the counter and stopped at the young assistant's side. Squatting, she studied the woman's pale face and figured her to be somewhere in her early twenties. 'A drink won't help if she's struggling to breathe. Hi, there. What seems to be wrong?'

The young assistant gave Gila a shaky smile and gasped, 'It's…an asthma attack. I'll…be…all right in…a moment.'

'Where's your reliever inhaler?' Leo asked, joining them. Squatting on the woman's opposite side, he also ran his expert gaze over her, silently searching for clues for how bad the attack was.

She lifted her hand and showed them both the blue inhaler she clutched.

'How many puffs have you taken?' Leo quizzed, his tone relaxed and patient. Though Gila guessed he was mentally working through and ticking off his internal doctor's list. The one every trained medic used when dealing with a new medical situation. Going through a pre-set format of questions and observations as he calmly attempted to make a diagnosis and subsequent decision for the best treatment to give to the patient.

'Nine…' The woman gasped. 'It doesn't seem…to be working.'

'It's not making much difference?' Gila asked, turning to Leo. The woman's breathing continued to worsen. If the reliever inhaler wasn't doing its job, then it was best to get further medical help via the hospital.

Gila gently grasped the woman's hand and quietly reassured her. 'My husband is a doctor and I'm a midwife. We're going to help you, okay? I'm Gila and this is Leo. Can you tell me your name?'

'Kate.' The young woman wheezed before taking a last puff from her inhaler.

Gila smiled. 'Well, Kate, do you mind if my husband and I quickly check your vital signs? I'm sure you're used to doctors troubling and fussing at times like this, right?'

She nodded, giving her agreement, and for the next few moments between them Leo and Gila checked Kate's pulse, level of response, her nails and finally her breathing, which was still very laboured.

'How long have you suffered with asthma?' Leo asked as he finished his last check.

'Since…a toddler,' Kate replied.

'Do you know what triggered this attack?' Gila asked, aware sometimes an attack transpired because of environmental and emotional influences. If the problem was still present, it could be preventing the young woman's breathing from improving.

The woman glanced at her colleague, then whispered, 'Perfume. There was…a customer…just now…wearing…a ton… I served her.…'

'That's it, slow, deep breaths,' Gila coaxed, wanting to ease Kate's struggle when talking, but also needing information about what had set off the attack and whether it was still a risk to Kate.

Leo nodded and made a decision. 'Right, Kate. I think we need to call an ambulance to transfer you to the local hospital.'

The woman frowned and started to argue. 'I can't…first day…won't look…good…boss will…be—'

Gila cut her off, not about to leave the woman in dire straits when she required further medical help. It was obvious Kate was tiring. 'I'm sure your boss will understand how important it is for you to go to the hospital, where they can regulate your breathing and monitor you. You realise the risks involved to your health if you don't get help, especially as your reliever inhaler isn't helping you.'

Her colleague stepped forward and nodded. 'Of course she must go. I'll clear it with the store manager. I'm sure he'll understand. He has a small daughter who suffers with asthma.'

'I'll ring for an ambulance,' Leo said, standing and pulling out his mobile phone from his jacket pocket and shifting several paces away. 'Breathe slowly and deeply, Kate. You know what to do. I'm sure this isn't your first time dealing with such a severe attack.'

Kate nodded and did her best to stay calm and do as Leo advised.

Gila continued to monitor Kate, searching the woman's face for any concerning grey-blueness around the lips, but, luckily, they showed only a little pale. With Leo on the phone, she asked, 'Kate, is there anyone you want me to call to let them know that you're going to the hospital?'

Kate produced her phone and quickly pulled up a number. Handing it over to Gila, she rasped, 'My…mum. She'll worry…if I don't arrive…home on time.'

Gila nodded and pressed 'call'. Placing the mobile to her ear, she waited for someone to answer. After a few rings a female voice finally spoke. 'Hello?'

'Hi, is this Kate's mum?' Gila enquired.

'Yes, it is,' Kate's mother replied. 'Who is this?'

'My name is Gila Wright. I'm with your daughter Kate at the baby department where she's working and I'm calling to inform you that unfortunately she has suffered a severe asthma attack.'

'Oh, my goodness,' the mother gasped. 'Is she okay?'

'My husband's a doctor and I'm a midwife, but we both feel it's best if Kate heads to hospital as her reliever inhaler isn't helping to ease her breathing. We've already called for an ambulance, but your daughter has asked me to let you know what is going on.'

'I—I…yes, oh, thank you. Do you know which hospital she is going to?'

Gila glanced up to see two paramedics strolling into the department looking completely alien amongst all the cute baby paraphernalia. 'The ambulance is here now. I'll just ask the paramedics.'

She quizzed one of the men as he passed, explaining how the patient's mother needed to know where to pick up her daughter. She relayed the information before bidding Kate's mother goodbye and handed back the mobile to the young woman.

'Your mother will meet you at the hospital,' she said, giving Kate's shoulder a comforting squeeze. Relieved that she'd finally agreed to further help. Another job could always be found, but a life couldn't. Once at the hospital, the doctors would soon aid and monitor her breathing. 'Everything will be fine now.'

'They got here quick,' Gila murmured to Leo as the paramedics took over Kate's care.

'Just around the corner, apparently,' Leo replied. 'Ideally placed for when the call came over the radio. This is the third asthma attack they've dealt with today.'

'Thank goodness they were close. Last

thing Kate needs is to be waiting ages for the ambulance to arrive.'

'Thank…you,' Kate gasped minutes later as the paramedics led her from the department.

'Our pleasure,' Leo said with a wave. Staring after the paramedics as the trio left the floor and headed into the store's main lift, he added, 'Well, that was unexpected.'

'It seems to be becoming a regular thing when you and I go out. Aunt Tom the other day and poor Kate today.'

'Curse of being medical practitioners, I suppose.' Leo sighed, placing an arm around her shoulders once again. The action both pleasant and relaxed. They'd always touched one another freely and easily during their marriage and she had missed it during their weeks apart. 'How about I buy you a cup of something warm and milky and include a sugary treat with it once we finish here?'

Her stomach rumbled at his offer and she smiled. Hunger dictating her answer to his suggestion. 'Sounds lovely.'

'But first,' he said, turning her back around, 'we've our baby's pram to buy. Let's do it quickly before another emergency occurs.'

Gila laughed, not complaining when Leo

steered her back over to the counter and the assistant still waiting to help them.

'So, the counsellor?'

The idea of Leo talking to someone—a stranger—sat odd with Gila. Especially now she'd had time to think it over. Ever since he'd mentioned it last night, questions had surfaced in her mind as she tried to imagine how it felt to visit a complete outsider and expose all your deeply hidden fears and feelings to them for an hour each week. In the medical profession seeking help of any kind was encouraged and championed, but to actually do so—for *Leo* to—secretly shocked Gila.

Leo leaned back in his chair and sighed heavily. The sound saying a thousand things without the need for words or syllables. Other diners surrounded them in the rooftop café, drinking and eating, chatting and catching up with friends and family. But Gila hardly noticed them or the background hum of their conversations. Her whole attention instead on the man sitting across the small table from her with a slight frown creasing his brow.

'Yes?' Leo asked, weariness creeping over his features at her query.

Gila stirred sugar into her large mug of hot chocolate and shifted closer to the table, wanting to keep their conversation as private as possible despite their busy background. Her curiosity pushed her to ask for details, specifics, anything that would help her understand. But how to query without upsetting or offending Leo?

'What made you go?' she asked, meeting his gaze. 'I mean, we suggest to our patients to do this sort of thing when we think it will help them, but often medics are the worst people for following their own advice. So what convinced you to visit a counsellor?'

Leo half chuckled and shrugged. 'Mainly because my boss, Dr Peters, threatened to sack me if I didn't visit someone. I'd lost you, so I didn't want to add my job too. And then once I went, it helped me to reflect on the situation with Jodie and see it differently. Rather than repeatedly beating myself up over the decisions I made at the time, the counsellor forced me to question what else I could have done. And the conclusion is there was nothing else I could do. Viewing the whole situation today, I honestly don't believe I would've reached that conclusion alone or at all.'

He took a sip of his coffee and continued, 'I'd spent so many years trying to push away feelings and anger over Jodie and her life, and I guess it all just built up until it refused to stay silent any longer. Jodie's death was just the pinnacle where it all broke through, I guess.'

'And you're happier now?' she probed curiously.

'No, not happier,' he said. 'Because to get to where I am, I lost you in the process. So no, I'm not happier, but I am calmer and more accepting that I'm not to blame, not really. That no matter how much I tried or what I gave, it would never have helped Jodie fight her own struggles. The parts of her were just too damaged.'

Gila reached across and grasped his hand, clutching it tightly. Glad he'd finally acknowledged the truth and found peace with it. 'You never were at fault, Leo. Not about your sister. Never that.'

He smiled softly and placed his other hand on top of hers. His thumb slowly stroking across her skin, causing it to tingle. A shiver of awareness shimmered over her wrist and up her arm.

Leo leaned forward and squeezed her hand, his skin warm against her own. 'Drink your hot chocolate. And then I think we should spend what's left of the afternoon at the pictures.'

'You want to go to the cinema?' she asked,

stunned by the suggestion. She'd half expected them to go their separate ways now they'd completed their shopping. Yet it appeared Leo wished to prolong their afternoon together.

'Yeah, why not. Fancy it?'

Yes, she really did. She nodded and smiled. 'I think I do.'

He tilted his head to one side and regarded her. 'It's what we did on our first date, wasn't it? Do you remember?'

She smiled and lifted her mug. Glancing at him over the rim, she replied, 'Of course I do. You chose a horror film and then spilt your popcorn all over the floor when one of the ghosts jumped out of the box in the cellar.'

'I never jumped,' he denied. 'My arm jerked, nothing more.'

She scoffed, not believing his excuse any more today than she had back then. 'At exactly the same time?'

He smirked. 'Damn muscle spasms. Never sure when they're going to happen. One moment you're absolutely fine, the next, *wham*, it hits you.'

She laughed and placed her mug down on the table. Wham was kind of how she'd felt the first time they'd met. One minute she'd taken in the unknown doctor offering his help during a woman's labour, and the next she'd fallen full heart in love with him.

Trouble was, she wasn't sure if a part of her didn't still feel the same way, no matter how much she desperately warned her tattered, beaten heart to protect against it. Because second chances might sound wonderful and achievable, but it still meant putting your heart back where it risked being hurt all over again. And she wasn't sure she would ever be brave enough to do that.

CHAPTER NINE

'GOOD MORNING.' LEO stepped into the kitchen
from outside, accompanied by a chilly blast
of early morning spring air. In one hand he
carried a brown paper bag and his car keys
dangled from the other. 'Sleep okay?'

Gila nodded and resumed spooning tea
leaves into the vintage china teapot. Her
movements fluid and relaxed. The initial tension that had throbbed between them during
the first few days had disappeared completely
after yesterday's trip to town, and being
around each other now felt more regular and
normal. Like old times, but not quite. Enough
to get them smoothly through the next few
days, though, she hoped.

And then what? her annoying internal
voice quizzed. At the moment, she couldn't
answer that question. There was still so much
to think about.

Tipping the last heaped teaspoon into the teapot, she said, 'Yes. You?'

'Like a baby,' he joked. 'Baby shopping is definitely a good cure for insomnia. I'll remember so in future.'

Gila screwed the lid back onto the tin and reached for the recently boiled kettle. From the corner of her eye she observed Leo as he opened a cupboard and withdrew a small plate, searching for obvious signs he wasn't sleeping well. What kept him awake these days? The unsettled state of their marriage, or did remaining stress from Jodie's death still haunt him? She wanted to ask, but faltered, not sure if he would tell her considering she'd refused to listen to him for so long.

But wasn't that exactly the problem that had plagued them before she left? The fact that she'd stepped away from asking uncomfortable and personal questions. Drew back from demanding answers, because she was half afraid to hear their subsequent replies. If she'd stayed and continued to prod and poke, would the depth of his grief and depression eventually have surfaced through his silence and become evident?

'What are you planning to do today?' Leo asked, placing the bag on the counter top. He leaned over to retrieve a second plate from the wooden rack above her head. The smell of fresh morning air and his spicy aftershave encircled her as he stretched close. Its crispness enticing her to lean into its invisible swirl.

She tilted her head to one side as she pondered her day's plans. Did he ask because he wished to include himself in them? The time they'd spent together yesterday was both fun and enjoyable. The film they'd watched at the cinema funny and light-hearted. Did he seek more togetherness or was she just secretly hoping so?

'I figured I would try and finish the blanket I'm knitting and then go through the list I made and see if I've forgotten anything for the baby.'

'Sounds a good idea.'

Popping the lid on the teapot, she gave it a swirl, careful not to spill liquid from the spout, and then glanced at Leo. Placing the teapot down again, she turned to him. 'Leo, about yesterday.'

He pulled a pastry slice scattered with almonds and white icing from the brown bag and dropped it onto a plate. 'Yes?'

'I just want to say how much I appreciate you telling me about the counsellor and Jodie. I realise it isn't easy for you—'

He reached out and grasped her hand, staring down at it thoughtfully before he spoke. 'You're right, it's not. I find it hard to open up and just let everything out. Even though it's all inside, saying the words out loud is tough.'

'But it helps?' she asked. 'Talking?'

He nodded. 'Yeah. After years of suppressing stuff, it does. I just wish I'd tried it before you left. Maybe then things between us wouldn't have gone the way they did. I've always admired the way you've always spoken so honestly about your own childhood. Never hiding anything. I guess being raised by parents who believe appearances are more important than the truth they conceal has unfortunately left its mark on me.'

Squeezing his fingers, she encouraged, 'If it makes you feel happier, then keep letting it out. It's obviously working for you.'

'What if what I say makes no sense?' he quizzed, self-consciously.

'If it's what's in your heart, then it will,' she reassured him. 'And it doesn't matter as long as you get it out.'

He nodded, then slowly met her gaze. 'I loved Jodie, but when you've spent so many years protecting and helping someone, which in the beginning you're happy to do because you care for them, but the longer it goes on and nothing helps or the situation never changes, that love dies inch by inch and re-sentment and tiredness replaces it. The simple reality was that no one could help Jodie. Not me, not you, not anyone.'

'I see,' she said, her heart breaking at the sadness clouding his eyes. Admitting such a bleak truth must be hard. No matter how much a person might want to fight for the hope of improvement and change, sometimes it turned out to be a struggle that could never be won.

Leo sighed, letting go of her hand to roll one shoulder. 'I'm probably not explaining any of this very well.'

'You are,' she soothed, instantly missing his contact. Before she would have reached out and pulled his hand back, but now she hesitated over doing such a thing.

'Really?'

She nodded. 'I've shared with you before how much I hated the way my father dragged me to yet another town or a different country. What he viewed as adventure, I perceived as hell. I never understood his excessive need to travel somewhere new. He loved new sounds, new people and new sights. Whereas I craved the regular pattern of school terms and sleeping in the same comfortable safe bed every night. In the end, I couldn't stand it and begged Art to give me a home. I think it broke my father's heart when I told him I didn't want to live or travel with him any more. He barely spoke to me again, and when he died of heart failure in Africa it was too late. He just never understood how I felt.'

'Families can be tough work sometimes, can't they? Always putting their own wants and wishes first,' Leo mused. 'I'm barely speaking to my parents.'

'Aunt Tom mentioned you'd fallen out with them.'

'She did?' Leo asked, then sighed. 'They blame me for Jodie's death. The fact that I didn't find some cure to turn her back into the perfect and presentable daughter they'd imagined having is just another disappointment they hold against me.'

'That's ridiculous,' Gila said. 'You're a doctor, not a magician. Addiction doesn't work like that.'

'I know it doesn't. But in their eyes failure is unacceptable. No matter whose or the reason why.'

'Surely you explained to them—'

Leo snorted. 'They refused to listen. The same way they always dismiss anything that doesn't fit into their nice orderly lifestyle. My parents have never dirtied their own hands when it involved Jodie and me. I don't think either of my parents ever changed a nappy or comforted us when we were ill. Why do the menial tasks of parenthood when they can pay someone else to do it?'

'But those are the most important jobs, aren't they?' Gila argued. 'Being there for your child whenever they need you. Kissing their hurts and loving them.'

'They are. And the reason my parents never bothered to visit Jodie in hospital before her death wasn't because they couldn't get a flight over in time.'

'It wasn't?'

'No, it was because they said there was no point since she was in a coma and wouldn't know if they were there or not. Truth is, they didn't want the embarrassment of the hospital staff knowing they were the parents of an addict.'

'Oh, Leo,' Gila sighed. 'Why didn't you tell me?'

He looked away. 'Because I didn't want to drag you into it.'

Gila desperately longed to wrap her arms around him and absorb some of his pain. It throbbed so intensely from him, she ached to soothe it. Instead, she said, 'Your parents are fools. And I'm glad you found help, Leo. I really am.'

She meant it. Where she hadn't pulled Leo from the pit of his grief, someone else had managed to succeed. Despite the knowledge leaving her feeling completely incompetent as a partner and a wife, she was grateful that he'd found the help he required from someone.

Lifting his gaze, he found hers. 'For years I tried to hold Jodie up and not let her sink completely, but it was hard and tiring. Juggling my career and life while trying to shore her up whenever she needed it. Helping her and knowing that if I didn't nobody else would. That no one in her life loved her the same. But when we found out you were pregnant, I decided I couldn't do it any more. I just didn't want to. And I didn't trust her to behave around you. She already begrudged your place in my life and heart. And you and the baby need all of me, not just a share. So I told Jodie that if she didn't try to get clean for good, then she was on her own.'

'How did she take it?' Gila asked softly.

'Badly.' He sighed heavily and confessed, 'After I gave her the ultimatum, I felt ashamed.'

Confused, she asked, 'Ashamed? Why?'

'Because when she refused, I felt an overpowering sense of relief. Like something huge and crushing had been removed and, honestly, it felt so good. For the first time since she was born, I didn't have to be responsible for her and her problems or wants. I could finally concentrate on just us and the baby. Something I *wanted* to do, rather than something I felt I *had* to do.'

Leo shut his eyes, recalling that day with familiar old regret. Jodie had reacted the same way she always had when denied her own way. She'd hated the idea that she and her issues were not the most important thing in his life. The truth was Jodie had been dramatic and selfish. Only ever concerned with herself. She'd accused him of hating her. Of letting her down. Said *he* was the real reason that she took drugs. That if he'd been a nicer, more caring brother, then she would have had a better life. If he had done more to help her, loved her more, then she would have had everything he did.

But it was all lies and wishful thinking. Jodie had made her own mistakes and never wanted to face them or admit that she was at fault. If anyone quizzed her or tried to make her see the truth, she turned on the tears and cried. Threw a tantrum and then sulked rather than see and accept that others saw things differently. She was bone-deep self-centred and jealous and it was always someone else's fault.

And then she turned her bitterness and anger onto his unborn child. The hateful words she said that day a poisonous memory Leo would never forget or forgive. One thing to tell him that he was a rotten brother who'd make an even worse father, but to wish harm to his child was something no decent person ever did or wished. Anger and resentment were no excuse for what she'd said, especially when it had later stirred up doubts inside him. Deep, dark worries that questioned whether he was capable of becoming a decent and loving father, if he couldn't save his own sister.

'But then she overdosed,' Gila reflected quietly. Breaking through his recollections.

'Yes.' Less than two months later he'd received a call from a colleague at the hospital informing him that Jodie was in a coma. By letting go of his sister and wanting a life for himself, he'd sent her hurtling towards a grave. At least that was how it had felt for a while. When the uncertainties and Jodie's last angry remarks had continued to echo loud and strong in his ears during the weeks after her death.

'I wish I'd known,' Gila said, grabbing his arm.

Leo frowned and quizzed, 'Why?'

'Because sometimes I felt shut out of your relationship,' Gila admitted. 'I'd always envisioned an in-law would become a close friend, but when that didn't happen with Jodie, I felt excluded from your bond. I longed to be a part of you two, but, no matter how I tried to help, I couldn't find a way in.'

Leo shook his head. 'I never meant for you to feel that way. I simply wished to keep you clear from all the chaos of Jodie at her worst. I wanted you and I to stay free from the added drama. We—our marriage—were a sanctuary filled with light and joy. I didn't want to spoil that.'

'If you'd just told me,' she said, not able to hide the reproach in her voice, 'I would have understood.'

He shrugged and nodded. 'I know that now. I made a lot of mistakes and not talking to you is my deepest regret. I suppose I gave into fear and let it control me. Half convinced that I had pushed Jodie to her death, and worried that I'd lose you and your respect if you ever discovered what I'd done. Which is ironic when you think how I lost you anyway by not telling you.'

She lowered her hand. 'I didn't know what to do when you drifted away from me.'

Leo groaned. 'I'm so sorry, Gila. Even though I could see what I was doing, I just couldn't stop and was terrifi—'

The sudden violent jerk of the boat prevented Leo from finishing. Instead he watched in horror as Gila went flying into the cupboards on the opposite side of the small galley kitchen before he could stop her.

'Gila!'

'What the…?' Gila gasped as intense pain shot through her stomach. Grasping the counter to steady herself, she cradled her stomach. Her instinct to protect the child inside her body stronger than any concern for herself. Wincing, she tried to straighten and catch her breath.

Leo reached for her, pulling her from her spot by the cupboard and into his arms. Clasping her in his warm embrace as though he feared a further attack from outside and aimed to shelter her from it and any additional injury. His automatic reaction to protect and keep her safe pleased and reassured Gila.

'Are you okay? Did you hurt yourself?' he demanded, his hands going to her bump.

'I'm fine, I think,' she said, reluctantly pulling back from his hold. She didn't want to. She'd rather stay secure in his arms until the shaking and trembling scrambling through her body ceased. But their relationship was already so confused and complicated, muddled to the point of total confusion, that to allow herself to indulge in things that threatened to make it more complex would be foolish and completely wrong for both of them.

'I hit my hip and stomach against the cupboard. It hurt for a moment, but it's subsiding now,' she said.

Leo immediately touched the mentioned area. His examination gentle and comforting as his fingers moved over the still throbbing tender spot. 'And the baby? Is the baby okay? The way you went flying across the space and smacked into the cupboard I thought...' His words trailed off but she understood his meaning. She wasn't the only one shaken from the unexpected bang against the boat's side.

Placing a reassuring hand on his arm, she smiled up at him. Her heart tugging at the genuine fear and distress shadowing his gaze. Turning his normally brown eyes to almost black. Quickly, she soothed, 'None the worse, I promise. We're both fine, Leo. Honestly. Just a touch wobbly and stunned.'

'Are you sure?' he persisted, rubbing his hand over the curve of her stomach again. As though, by caressing it, he could comfort both her and the baby. Guard them from the unforeseen hazards in the world.

She nodded and attempted to draw some normality into the moment, because if she didn't force her thoughts to move in a different direction, she might do something stupid like kiss her estranged husband fully on the mouth. 'Do you think another narrowboat hit into us?'

Moving narrowboats banging into moored ones often occurred during holiday periods and summer, when holidaymakers hired a boat for the first time and took to the water with very little training or skill. Usually plates or cups became the casualties of such comings together, but this time it was her pregnant body that took the full brunt of someone's thoughtless and unintentional mistake.

Leo frowned and his mouth thinned. With a gentle squeeze to her side, he declared, 'I'm going to go and find out. I won't be a minute. Perhaps you should sit down.'

He disappeared before Gila could stop him. Wrapping her arms around herself, she tried to calm the still present shaking. Moments later, she heard the low mumble of Leo's deep voice talking with someone outside. No, it sounded as if he was scolding someone. Sometimes the doctor's authoritative tone worked for situations other than when dealing with a disruptive or confused patient.

Gila shakily finished making her tea and sat down on the sofa. Holding the warm mug with both hands, she slowly breathed in deeply. Despite her assurances to Leo, the knock had shocked her and her hip still smarted from its forceful impact into the cupboard. Though the backache she'd woken up with that morning bothered her more. Different in sensation from the normal pregnancy aches she'd experienced for the last few days. She'd done her best not to dwell on it, but it wasn't easy when the area throbbed constantly. Aunt Tom's words floated through her mind again, but she quickly dismissed them. This baby wasn't going to be early. The old woman wasn't a medical expert or a midwife. She hadn't spent years studying the subject. She was just a sweet old woman who'd worked at the local library before the council had closed it during a round of cutbacks in the early nineties.

Taking a sip of her milky tea, she glanced up when Leo returned, his expression grimmer than when he'd left. The slamming of the door behind him an indication his mood hadn't improved after his conversation outside.

'Is our boat still in one piece?' she asked curiously. Be just her luck if the narrowboat suffered serious damage and required her to move somewhere else for the rest of the week. Where she'd go, she didn't want to consider.

'Fortunately,' Leo said, sitting down next to her. 'And to add to this morning's drama, apparently a lorry has just overturned and blocked the canal path's entrance. Thanks to a spilt cargo of oranges we're all trapped here on our boats, with no other way out for some time.'

She laughed, glad for the distraction from the pains of her body. 'Oh, dear. It appears to be one of those days, doesn't it? Good thing we both have today off *and* that you managed to get to the cake shop before the lorry's accident.'

He agreed, then searched her face. 'Are you sure you're all right? No pain or twinges? Cuts or stings?'

She smiled and gave his hand a pat. 'Leo, I'm fine. At the most I'll probably end up with a couple of bruises to show for my unexpected flight across the kitchen.'

Leo gave her a wry glance. 'Well, you may be fine, but I'm not sure I am. All I keep recalling is the way you banged into the cupboard. Our son or daughter must be wondering what is going on. Lying there all contented one second, the next thing bam!'

She chuckled, the concern in his eyes too sweet to resent. Perhaps this was their way forward. A close and comfortable friendship instead of the lingering anger and disappointment of their marriage. For their child's sake they had to form a platonic relationship if nothing else.

She rubbed the top of her stomach. 'Luckily he or she is well protected in there.'

'Thank God,' Leo said. 'With the canal entrance blocked and no other way out for at least half a mile, the last thing we need is a medical emergency.'

Gila murmured in agreement, ignoring the discomfort in her back. It was just pregnancy aches, nothing else. Just normal third-trimester niggles and twinges. And definitely nothing to do with labour.

* * *

The dull ache in Gila's lower back hadn't eased by late afternoon and neither a bath nor lying flat out on the normally comfortable bed helped ease it. For the umpteenth time she turned onto her side, hugging a pillow close, in the faint hope of finding a smidgen of relief from the persistent torment.

Just stupid pregnancy discomfort and certainly no reason to panic and start thinking crazy thoughts. First babies always arrived late. They really did. Occasionally mothers would even require inducing to get a way too contented baby to give up their comfortable home of nine months and join the world outside. Yes, the odds were definitely piled in that direction. This baby wasn't coming yet. The uncomfortable feeling was nothing but the delightful joys of late pregnancy and nothing more. There'd been no signs that her pregnancy would differ from most other first babies. She just needed to relax and stop thinking the worst. If Aunt Tom hadn't mentioned the baby arriving early, then she wouldn't be having any doubts. It was all the old woman's fault, muttering ill-informed, old-wives'-tales nonsense. At least she'd spared Gila the ring-dangling-off-a-piece-of-string theatrics in an effort to guess the baby's sex.

Leo stepped into the room then paused. His gaze slowly running over her. Folding his arms, he said, 'You're glaring. Is something bothering you?'

Yes, everything. Pain made her seriously grumpy and she hated being in a bad mood. It made her even more irritated. 'It's my back. It's really hurting and I can't get comfortable no matter how I lie.'

He mumbled something under his breath and drew closer. Sitting down on the bed, he asked, 'Do you want me to rub your back? It might help.'

The offer sounded nice and the thought of his fingers magically massaging her tender sore muscles had her nodding in agreement. 'If you don't mind.'

She tried not to sound too eager, but she longed for his strong digits to alleviate her pain. She was desperate for it to go or at least lessen, and if he achieved a few moments of respite, she was beyond caring about any rightness or wrongness of whether he should be doing it. She just craved some relief.

Leo smiled softly and coaxed, 'Why don't you roll over onto your other side for me?'

Without a word, she did as he suggested,

groaning when his hand slowly stroked over her hip before moving lower towards her throbbing spine. She sucked in a breath, as he pushed down the waistband of her leggings and caressed her bare flesh. 'Is this where it hurts?'

She groaned and purred, as his thumbs tenderly pushed into her flesh and moved in small circles. 'Oh, yes. Just there.'

Leo chuckled and massaged the area for several minutes, easing the tension out of the tight muscles. His fingers lightly resting against her lower back. His touch firm but gentle. 'Does that help?'

'It feels *so* good,' Gila moaned, snuggling her face into the soft pillow to muffle a whimper of pleasure that escaped. But after several hours without a break from the constant pain, the momentary relief felt heavenly and lovely. 'So very nice. The NHS should hire you out to pregnant women. You'd be booked up for years.'

He snorted at the idea, and asked, 'You'd give me a reference, then?'

Gila silently gave the idea more consideration. Leo's hands all over other women when everyone knew that pregnancy hormones often increased a woman's sex drive. The thought of amorous women enjoying her husband's soothing and wonderful backrub suddenly horrified her. His hands weren't going anywhere. They were hers to keep and use.

'Actually, it's a terrible idea,' she determined, realising only seconds later that she'd said the words out loud.

He leaned over, his breath warm and carrying the faint whiff of coffee when he spoke. 'It is?'

'Yes,' she replied, burying her face further into the pillow without smothering herself. Not wanting him to see the flush of embarrassment warming her cheeks. Such honest thoughts were best kept to herself.

'Why is that?' he teased, his tone indicating he had guessed the reason for her sudden change of mind. His fingers increased their pressure, extracting another moan of pleasure from her.

'Oh, God, that is nice,' she groaned. Reluctant to confess the idea of him touching other women sent her stupidly possessive. No, she didn't intend to admit a thing. His ego would grow to gigantic proportions if she did.

'Because...' she hedged, searching for another plausible reason—one that didn't make her sound like a jealous wife. Because she wasn't jealous. She just didn't like the thought of Leo touching other pregnant women when his hands had far more important tasks to do as a doctor. Because to be jealous meant she still held feelings for the man and she wasn't sure what they were, and she refused to explore them in case she found the answer and didn't like it.

'Ow!' Gila gasped, her thoughts scattering as a new, different pain, unconnected to her back, ran across her stomach. Was that a contraction? She stared at the cotton pillowcase, once again glad Leo couldn't see her face from his angle.

'What's wrong?' he asked, his hands pausing as he waited for an answer. One hand holding her hip. 'Did I hurt you?'

'No,' she denied, trying to keep her voice steady and normal-sounding. Better to keep quiet until she'd worked out what was going on with her body and exactly what that last pain was. No reason to concern Leo yet.

'You gasped as though in pain. Are you sure you're okay?'

'Absolutely,' she lied. Probably nothing more than Braxton Hicks, the pre-contractions all women experienced as their bodies readied for labour. Unquestionably nothing to worry over. She was *not* in labour. She wasn't.

'Perhaps you should try to sleep,' Leo suggested, replacing the band of her leggings over the area he'd just massaged. His fingers paused as though hesitant to break their connection.

'Is the path still blocked with oranges?' Gila asked, trying to sound more curious than desperate.

Leo patted her hip. 'Yeah, apparently there's a bad accident on the other side of the city, which takes precedence over this one. It could be several more hours before the recovery truck arrives to clear our entrance.'

Gila swallowed and pushed the terrifying feeling climbing up her throat back down. Not normally prone to panic, she forced her thoughts to settle. It was just Braxton Hicks. Nothing else. Just her body preparing itself for birth. One that would happen sometime in the next few weeks. Because there was no chance that this baby was on its way today. Absolutely none.

Oh, God, there was no denying it, even though Gila had frantically tried. The pains shooting across her stomach and in her back were definitely more than just practice contractions. As a midwife she knew about these things. She'd helped other women through their own labour and recognised the signs, even if a very big part of her had refused to admit it.

Shuffling to the bed's edge, she swung her feet to the floor and padded to the door. Leaving the bedroom, she headed for the sitting room, pausing on the threshold as she pondered the best way to announce the news to Leo, who sat reading on the sofa and hadn't yet noticed her.

Silently, she ran through several different options.

Leo, I'm in labour.

Leo, the baby is coming.

Guess what, Leo? In a few hours we're going to be proud parents.

Hey, Leo, how do you fancy spending your day off at the maternity unit? That's if we can get there considering the path is blocked and we're kind of trapped here.

She closed her eyes and shook her head.

Gila, just stop messing around and tell the man. It's not as though you created the situation. No, that was down to nature and their child. Opening her eyes, Gila coughed to get her husband's attention. 'Leo?'

'Hey, you didn't sleep long,' Leo said, tossing the medical journal he was reading to one side and getting to his feet.

'I kept waking up,' she said, figuring it best not to just announce the news.

He folded his arms and regarded her. A flicker of worry in his eyes. 'Is your back still hurting?'

'Yeah, but…well, it's not like normal back pain.'

That was good, Gila. Several obvious hints should ease the telling.

'Really? What do you think it is?' he asked, raising an eyebrow.

'I wonder if it might be…' She trailed off, hoping he'd catch on, but the lack of suspicion in his expression that her pain might be something more serious than random aches killed all hope. And he called himself a doctor.

'Yes?' he queried.

'Oh, dear,' she gasped, her eyes widening as another contraction ripped across her lower body. She glanced at her watch, horrified to see the contractions were getting closer in time to one another.

Leo reached out and grabbed her arms. 'Gila, what is it? What's wrong?'

'Well, I'm pretty sure that there's a chance I'm experiencing contractions,' she said, trying to soften the news, but knowing she failed dismally when she heard his sharp intake of breath and saw the startled widening of his eyes. 'I've been having them for a while.'

'What?' Leo repeated sharply. 'How long? Not since the boat hit us?'

'No, sometime after.'

'Why didn't you tell me?' he demanded.

'I wasn't sure—' she started.

'But you're a midwife,' he declared, placing his hands on his hips. With a confused frown, he asked, 'How can you not know? You're the expert.'

'But I've never given birth, though,' she reasoned back. 'Yes, I've read all the textbooks and helped out practically, but, in case you've forgotten, I've never gone through the actual physical process myself. It's one thing to read and learn about it from books and stuff, but another to do it. You know, a person can only gain so much understanding from helping women in childbirth. I mean, as a doctor you're aware of what occurs during an amputation, but it doesn't mean you know exactly what it feels like to have one.'

'You're right,' he agreed, then asked, 'You don't think these pains are simply practice contractions?'

Gila almost laughed at Leo's hopeful expression. So similar to her own for the last few hours. But there was no more ignoring or denying the truth. This baby was coming no matter how early or inconvenient it might be for them.

'No, I'm sure it's the real thing—' She stopped, her mouth falling open and her eyes widening in horror.

'What's wrong?' Leo demanded.

Colour flooded her cheeks and she shook her head. 'Nothing.'

'Gila,' he said more gently.

She sighed and slowly glanced down, taking in the puddle of amniotic fluid now soaking her feet and oozing into the carpet. 'Looks like my waters have just broken.'

Leo's gaze shot downwards, before he swallowed hard and agreed, 'Hell, Gila. You really *are* in labour.'

CHAPTER TEN

GILA'S STOMACH DROPPED as reality leached into her brain. They were stuck on the narrowboat and she was in labour, and all she could think to do was wrap herself into Leo's body and hide. Snuggle into his chest and close her eyes until it all went away.

But she couldn't do any of that, because this baby wasn't playing around and she and Leo were—who knew what? God, why were relationships so hard to work out and keep straight? Perhaps it would be best if they just forgot the past for the next few hours and concentrated on getting through their child's birth. Together. As a couple but not a couple. Just two close friends, helping each other out. Because despite all her training and knowledge, she felt the same as any other female in labour. A tiny bit anxious and worried over what was to come in the following hours.

'The recovery truck is still at the site of the

other accident. Once it gets here, it will take a while to shift it to a safe position before they can remove it,' Leo said, placing a towel over the puddle at her feet. 'But we probably have plenty of time before we need to leave for the maternity unit.'

'Then we'll wait,' she pronounced with more conviction than she felt. Her labour would in all probability last for hours. First babies were rarely quick births. Everything would be fine. The blocked entrance would be a blip they'd laugh over later from the comfort of a hospital bed. No reason to panic. Seriously, there wasn't. None at all.

'Okay, then can I get you anything?' Leo asked.

Shaking her head, she sucked in a calming breath. Determined to act tranquil and chilled. No hysterical mother-to-be was she. Oh, no. Mother Nature could learn from her. So, ignoring her racing heart and the nerves busily rock-and-rolling in her stomach, she smiled brightly. 'No, thank you. I'm good.'

Leo walked over to the sofa and started throwing cushions in random directions. One flew over his shoulder and landed on the floor by her feet. 'Perhaps you should sit down.'

Gila crouched and retrieved the cushion from the floor, biting her lower lip to stop herself from laughing at Leo. But honestly when a person stopped and considered the situation it was funny. Separated couple stuck on their narrowboat, dealing with the onset of wife's unexpected labour.

Another cushion dropped off the sofa and onto the floor. What exactly was he doing? If she didn't know him so well, she'd believe he was rattled. But Leo never—'

Ow, that hurt.

She grimaced and clutched the cushion tight against her body as another contraction hit.

Gasping, she concentrated on breathing through the pain. Trying to recall everything she told her expectant mothers during their labour. Something pacifying and comforting. But no matter how hard she focused, her mind refused to conjure up the words of advice she'd spoken hundreds of times in the past, and instead fixated on the pain and nothing else.

With a quick glance at Leo still beating cushions into haphazard new positions, she checked her watch. Oh, dear, the contractions were getting closer. This baby wasn't playing. It appeared their child was eager to greet the world and it wasn't waiting for the vehicle-recovery team to turn up. Perhaps it would be best to consider the possibility that they were not going to make it to the hospital and instead ready themselves for having the baby here at home.

'Will you rub my back, please?' she asked, hoping to distract Leo. If she didn't, he might start rearranging the furniture next. Wasn't it supposed to be the mother who displayed the nesting urge, not the father?

Leo straightened and rushed to her side. 'Yes, of course. Where does it hurt?'

Another contraction hit Gila hard. Yep, definitely getting closer. Groaning, she did her best to breathe through the pain. First-time babies were supposed to come on time, late even, certainly not early. And not this quick once they decided to. Why couldn't one thing follow the book? Was this a sign of this child's personality? Did it intend to always ignore the rules of life and do its own thing?

'You're doing great,' Leo encouraged, rubbing her back and holding her hand as she blew through the contraction. 'That's it, deep breaths and—'

She was in agony and probably going to give birth here in their home, without any pain relief or familiar colleagues hanging around to help. Not even her own midwife. Just her and Leo. The two of them, and, yes,

they were capable and fully trained, but this
was the birth of *their* baby and that alone ren-
dered it different from any other.

Letting out a long sigh as the contraction
receded, Gila puffed away a stray strand of
hair from her face and glanced at the man
holding her. 'Ah, Leo.'

He continued to rub her back, but leaned
in. 'Yes, sweetheart?'

'I think we'd better get several blankets and
shake them out onto the floor.'

He frowned and repeated, 'Blankets?'

'Yes.'

His frown deepened. 'Are you cold?'

She almost laughed at the innocence of his
question. 'No, but I don't think our son or
daughter is going to wait until after the recovery truck arrives. My contractions are getting closer and closer. This baby is coming
soon and it looks like it is up to us to bring
this little one into the world.'

Every healthy trace of colour drained
from her husband's face, and he stammered,
'What? But your waters have only just broken.'

Gila sent him an encouraging smile. 'Yeah,
that sometimes happens. Childbirth likes to
liven things up occasionally with the unpredictable.'

'But—'

She grasped his hand tighter. 'We're professionals, Leo. We can do this. We've no other choice.'

'I guess—' he started.

'And giving birth is a beautiful and natural experience,' she said, repeating the words she always said to her mothers-to-be. She just hadn't expected her childbirth to be this natural, but, hey, life handed over the occasional surprise and a person had no choice but to face it.

'But it's *our* baby,' Leo stated, his hand tensing around her fingers.

She knew exactly what he meant. One thing to help strangers give birth, but completely different now they were the ones going through the whole procedure without any kind of medical back-up. 'I know.'

He swallowed hard, then asked, 'Are you worried?'

She glanced at him, desperate once again to throw herself into his arms and vanish. To submerge into his body and disappear. 'No, of course not,' she lied. When in truth, she was just a little bit petrified.

Leo gathered the blankets and other items Gila asked for. His mind spinning like a fairground ride dipping and diving all over as he struggled to concentrate on the chore and not the situation.

Gila was in labour. Apparently, she'd been having contractions for hours and never said a word. Not a single one. How had he missed the clues? Hadn't she complained about back-ache for the last day or so? And now they were stuck on the narrowboat with no way out, unless a person wanted to hike for half a mile to the next exit, or until both the lorry and the ruined fruit were scraped up from the road and removed.

Sinking onto the bed, he cradled his head in his hands. Nausea turning in his stomach. This couldn't happen and certainly not here. When women gave birth, especially for the first time, it was best they did so in a nice clean hospital, with all the specialist equip-ment on hand if things went wrong.

Went wrong? Where did that thought come from?

Leo stood and began to pace the floor of the small bedroom. God, what if something went wrong? It was possible. There was al-ways a chance the baby could become dis-tressed or it would be a difficult birth. What if the baby was breech? What if Gila haem-orrhaged? Saving her would be down to him alone. With no back-up or equipment how could he do that? How would he manage? With the road blocked, there was no way to get her and the baby to the safety of a hospital if they needed to in an emergency.

He groaned and buried his face in his hands again. It wasn't supposed to be like this. This was the day he'd looked forward to for months. The moment when their family grew from a duo into a trio. Not once had he imagined it would occur in their home, with only him to tend and help Gila through the birth. And he'd certainly never pictured they would still be in a romantic deadlock when doing it.

He swallowed the bitter acid taste coating his mouth and pushed all emotional thoughts to one side. He would not fall apart. He was a doctor from his fingernails to his toes. Some people even called him an excellent doctor. He faced and thrived in stressful situations. Never knowing what to expect each time he started a shift in A & E. And today Gila needed him. She was his emergency. He'd treat her the same as he would any other patient. They were both medical professionals with plenty of experience between them and, whatever happened, they'd find a way to cope. There was no other choice. Their child was determined to appear soon and nature would dictate everything from here, as it already was. He just had to hang around to keep things going smoothly.

Rubbing his face one last time, he quickly gathered everything they required, then changed his mind and deposited the items onto the small chair near the bed. No way was his wife giving birth on the lounge floor when she could do it on a comfortable bed. The actual bed where they'd conceived their child. Somehow it seemed the perfect place.

Women all over the world gave birth outside hospitals and they did it just fine. Frequently without the help or interference of a medic. He prayed it would be the same for Gila and their child. Together they would be able to do this.

Rushing back to the lounge where Gila was now sitting on the sofa breathing deeply, he said, 'Why don't we do this in the bedroom?'

Gila considered the question for a moment, then nodded. 'Yes, good idea. Much more relaxing. Better than spread out on the floor. But we'll need to cover the bed with something waterproof to save the mattress from getting ruined.'

Leo nodded then hurried back in the bedroom's direction, spending the next few minutes stripping the bed, before heading through the lounge and continuing on to the door outside.

'Where are you going?' Gila called out.

'There's an unopened tarp in the storage box. We can spread it over the bed before replacing the sheets. It might rustle a bit, but the mattress will stay stain-free and clean.'

Gila nodded and Leo disappeared outside, before returning minutes later with the tarp. In no time the bed was remade and ready for her.

Leo returned to Gila's side and gently helped her to stand. 'How are you doing, darling?'

'I'm fine,' she replied. 'You?'

'Great,' he lied. Perhaps it wouldn't hurt to head back outside and get an update on the lorry's expected arrival time.

'I think I'll have a quick shower,' Gila said, interrupting his racing thoughts.

A shower? She wanted a shower? What if the baby shot out while she was in there? Yes, he was a doctor, but childbirth wasn't his speciality. He could get her through the birth, but this was all Gila's expertise. He'd prefer she climbed into bed and stayed there, cutting down the risk of any unexpected surprises. If they were going to do this, couldn't they at least do it the simplest way?

'Do you think that's a good idea?' he asked. 'Can't we just head for the bed and stay there?'

She smiled slightly and shook her head. 'Leo, there's no reason why I can't move around or take a shower. It's good to keep moving. I've read a lot of studies on it. Besides, a shower will help me to relax. It's perfectly fine. We've loads of time before things pick up.'

'Okay,' he said, already deciding it would be the quickest drench under the hose she'd ever taken. 'If it's what you really want.'

She smirked and patted his chest. 'Everything is going to be fine. We can do this.'

Leading her to the bathroom, he helped Gila remove her top and leggings, before stepping back. 'Can you manage from here?'

She nodded, but stopped him when he turned to leave the room. 'Where are you going?'

He pointed towards the corridor. 'I'll wait in the hall until you've finished. Give me a shout if you want any help.'

'No, I want you to stay with me,' she said, the expectation and hope in her expression almost Leo's breaking point. Didn't the woman realise how close he hovered to the tip of anxiety?

He glanced longingly at the open bathroom door then back at Gila. Careful to keep his thoughts from his face, he asked, 'Are you sure it's what you want? You know, with the way things are between us.'

She hesitated for a moment, before saying, 'Please, Leo. I need you. Although I'm doing my best to stay calm, it's mostly an act. I'd really appreciate your support.'

Shame, anger and fresh determination pumped through him at her words. Softly spoken, they still had the power to annihilate him. Of course, she was scared, because this was her first time. Not giving himself a chance to question the sense of his actions, he tugged her to him and kissed the top of her head. 'I'm here, baby. I'm not going anywhere. I swear.'

'I can't do this,' Gila panted as yet another contraction ran through her body. She wanted to yell and weep all at the same time, but a part of her mind also told her to stay quiet and not make a fuss. She wasn't an outgoing, dramatic kind of person. The idea of screaming like a banshee was completely outlandish to her. But this had gone on long enough and now she was done.

'Gila?'

'Yes?' She winced at the sharpness of her tone, but found it impossible to regret. In the centre of the bed, on all fours, she tried to go with the pain, silently repeating to herself how childbirth was natural and survivable without the inclusion of drugs, but it wasn't easy when it hurt *so* much.

'Gila?' Leo repeated.

She sighed and rolled her eyes. Couldn't the man see she was busy? She didn't have the time or the desire for chit-chat. 'Yes?'

Leo touched her side and coaxed, 'You're doing beautifully, darling. Just a little longer. Your progress is perfect. Totally textbook, you'll be happy to hear.'

'How do you know it's going to be a little longer?' she demanded, suddenly angry. 'The baby's not inside you, is it? Doing its best to rip you to pie—'

Leo dunked back towards the bottom of the bed away from her complaining. Rubbing a comforting hand on her right leg, he soothed, 'But I am a doctor. So I outrank you even if you are doing all the work.'

'Pfft,' she dismissed. 'You mend broken bones and save people from life-threatening complications. You do *not* regularly bring new life into the world the way I do. *I'm* the baby expert here, Dr Wright. Understand? I make all the decisions. You just keep telling me what everything looks like down your end.'

He laughed and commented, 'Childbirth is making you grouchy, I see. Would you like more ice to suck on? Or do you fancy sitting up for a while? Shall I get the mirror from the bathroom so you can see what's happening, or do you trust me to do everything right?'

'I trust you,' Gila panted, because she did. Every question she asked, Leo answered with patience. When she demanded information, he gave it without hesitation. So far, he'd acted the perfect birthing partner. 'What I need is for this to be over and the baby in my arms.'

Leo again stroked his hand over her leg. 'You're doing really well and you're totally beautiful, too.'

'I'm not beautiful,' Gila dismissed crossly. 'I'm tired, on all fours and sweaty. In no realms of someone's imagination can I be viewed as anything but a hot, hormonal mess.'

'I think you're amazing,' he added, ignoring her complaints. 'And I'm so proud of you. You're doing brilliantly, Gila.'

'I'm being a nightmare patient, aren't I?' she suddenly sobbed, rubbing her hand against her forehead. 'I'm a terrible person, Leo. You're trying to help me and I'm being mean and angry and so flipping emotional and—'

'Our child's giving you a hard time,' Leo interrupted softly. 'You're allowed to be all of those. Besides, I've borne worse patients than you, trust me. You're in the minors league when it comes to awkwardness and bad behaviour.'

She snorted, wiping away a stupid tear. 'Thanks, I think.'

He smiled and rubbed her behind. 'But I've never had a patient as brave as you're being. Are you sure I can't fetch you more ice?'

'No, just stay here with me,' she begged as another contraction hit her. 'I need you.'

'Of course,' he said, reaching out to rub the base of her spine. Their purpose linked as their child fought in its journey towards life. 'We can get through this. Now a gentle push, that's it.'

Once the contraction eased, Leo checked her once more, struck speechless when he spotted the top of the baby's head. 'I can see the head. Oh, God, Gila. I can see the top of the baby's head.'

Gila chuckled. 'Really?'

'Yes, and it's amazing. A bit mucky, but amazing. Here comes the rest of it.'

'It's going to be soon,' Gila warned. 'I need to take a breath. Don't forget you'll need to check that the cord is not around the baby's neck.'

He shifted to the top of the bed and grabbed her hand and squeezed it. Smacking a loud, sloppy kiss to her damp forehead, he said, 'I'm ready when you are. Nice and slow, no rushing for this next part. The baby's head is out. You're doing really well.'

She laughed helplessly when he dashed away. 'I want to push.'

'Okay, but don't use too much pressure. The baby's coming. There's no sign of the cord. The shoulders are out, I'm ready to receive, sweetheart. Yes, that's it. Yes. Yes. Oh, my God, she's beautiful, Gila. Our daughter is utterly beautiful.'

CHAPTER ELEVEN

A FAINT ANGRY squall filled the bedroom moments later. Leo lifted his child and didn't bother to wipe his falling tears as he cradled her to his body. This angry, irritated miracle of a baby, created from his and Gila's love, was their child. And between them—together—they'd brought this wonderful small bundle into the world.

And she was perfect. Their sweet, precious daughter, only seconds born and a little mucky, was absolutely and completely perfect.

'Is everything okay?' a weary voice enquired from the other end of the bed.

Leo nodded, unable to find words, his throat and eyes full of more tears, and stepped closer to where Gila, exhausted, but beautiful, waited for them.

Grabbing a towel, he quickly wrapped it around the baby to keep her warm, before carefully laying her onto Gila's naked body, all the time careful to keep the cord, still attached to baby and placenta, free from tension. He would cut it in a second, but, first, it was time for mother and baby to get acquainted.

Gila gave him a tired smile, her eyes curious as she took in their daughter now placed against her stomach and breast. A tear of her own rolled slowly over her cheek. With shaky, hesitant fingers, she softly touched the baby's face. 'We have a little girl, Leo.'

Leo sat on the bed next to them. Aching to stretch out and hug the two most precious females in his life, but aware he still had work to do. There'd be plenty of time and occasions for cuddles. In fact, the rest of their lives.

'Oh, Leo. She's so...' Gila's words faded off as she stared at her baby. Love and wonder shining from her, as she gently stroked a finger across a precious cheek.

'Isn't she?' he agreed, placing his arm around Gila's shoulders. Together they silently took in the marvel of their newborn daughter. No words needed as they acquainted themselves with this longed-for stranger, who, since pushing her way early into the world, was now and would always be the centre of their lives.

Gila rubbed a light finger over the baby's hand. 'Look at how tiny her fingers are. Oh, Leo. Her nails are minuscule. I never imagined I would ever experience this moment. I always thought I would be alone in life. Until I met you.'

Leo gave into the urge and slipped his other arm around the baby, where Gila held her. Fresh tears fell, but he ignored them, too. For the first time in many months he was happy and he meant to enjoy it. Here with his wife and daughter. The one place he truly wished to stay. 'She's adorable, isn't she?'

There were no words good enough to describe their daughter. Beyond adorable or astonishing. Just perfect and theirs. How on earth they'd managed to create a child so breathtaking, he didn't know, but he thanked all the saints for gifting her to them.

'She looks like you,' Gila whispered, lightly rubbing the dark wisps of their daughter's hair.

'Really?' He frowned, not seeing it. Surely not. The baby was beautiful and he definitely wasn't. Rugged, some people liked to call him, but he just saw the same old beaten-up face he'd always owned, whenever he looked in a mirror.

'I think she resembles you more,' he said,

touching the baby's lower lip. His heart melted as his daughter tried to capture his finger with her mouth. 'Especially her mouth. Such a pretty one, isn't it? Just like yours.'

Gila smiled and continued to gaze at their daughter. 'Perhaps she simply looks like herself? A mixture of us, but totally individual.'

Leo liked that idea. Made by them, but original. 'Yep, I think you're right. Anyone looking at her can see she's amazing and unique. Shall I give her a quick wash, before you try feeding her?'

Gila nodded. 'Good idea. There's a blue bag in the bottom of the wardrobe at my uncle's. It contains baby stuff and a few newborn outfits. Though she's pretty long despite being a few weeks early, the all-in-ones should fit.'

Leo leaned over and gave into the urge before he stopped himself. Closing his eyes, he kissed Gila fully on the mouth, lingering for several long seconds before pulling away. He loved this woman and he hoped she understood exactly how much from that kiss. 'Thank you for our daughter.'

She smiled back and whispered, 'Thank you, too.'

Leo quickly dealt with the cord and placenta. Helping Gila to the chair, he quickly changed the sheets, before easing her and baby back into the bed.

Gathering all the dirty linen, he glanced at the woman and child sitting in the centre of the bed. His family. His girls.

Gila looked up and smiled at him. 'I guess despite everything we did something right.'

He nodded. 'We did. I'll go and get the bag from your uncle's place.'

Stepping outside the narrowboat, Leo paused and glanced up at the sky. Somehow, he had to put his marriage back together. He didn't want to be just friends or polite acquaintances with Gila. He craved more. He wanted his family living with him.

Tilting his head further back, he whispered, 'I'm a daddy, sis. I've a daughter and she's incredible.'

Leo wrapped the soft knitted cream blanket around their daughter and walked over to the bed.

'Make sure to hold her head—' Gila stopped and winced, knowing she didn't need to tell Leo what to do. The gentle, careful way he held and tended to the baby's needs showed he was more than capable. 'Sorry, I just…she's so dear and I want to be a help.'

Leo grinned. 'You're a protective new

mum, you're allowed to fuss. But I know what I'm doing. Besides, you did all the work bringing her into our lives, enjoy a minute's rest while she lets you.'

Gila sighed and leaned back against the clean pillow he'd switched when he changed the bedding earlier. The man hadn't stopped since their little one's arrival. Not only had he been the best stand-in midwife, Leo had helped her birth the placenta, cleaned her and the bed, and had just finished bathing their daughter. Without doubt a human dynamo of a man.

'Of course you do. Thanks, Leo. For everything.'

'My pleasure. Hey, I did the easy work. You're the one producing miracles today. Besides, can't have either of you going for a check-up at the hospital all messy, can we?'

Her second sigh filled the room as she snuggled into the pillows behind her back. 'I suppose it's best to get checked out.'

'If you want to stay home, you can, but I think all your friends at the maternity unit are hoping to see both you and baby. They were very excited when I phoned in and told them the news.'

She grinned. 'No, we'll go. We can grab

some takeaway on the way home. Besides, I want to show off our baby girl.'

Leo chuckled and rocked their whimpering daughter. Washed, dressed and, by the sounds of complaint coming from her, more than ready for a feed. 'Have you thought of any names?'

Content, Gila shrugged. 'A few. You?'

Leo bent over and placed their daughter down onto the mattress, close to the foot of the bed. Reaching for the stethoscope he'd fetched at the same time as Gila's baby bag, he placed one end in his ears and then blew on the other end to warm the metal, before bending over his wriggling baby.

'What are you doing?' Gila frowned as Leo partly unwrapped the blanket and pressed the stethoscope's end to their child's chest.

He straightened slightly and turned his head Gila's way. 'Thought I'd give our daughter a quick check over. So…names? How about Arabella?'

Gila tilted her head to one side and pondered the name. 'Arabella Wright. I like it. Actually, I love it. What about a middle name?'

Leo frowned and replaced the stethoscope back on the same spot on the baby's chest and listened once more. His frown deepening as he shifted the instrument slightly without saying a word.

'What's the matter?' Gila asked, seeing his concerned expression. She knew Leo well enough to know when he was troubled over something. Tautness radiated from his body so strongly that she could practically feel it pulsating across the space between them.

'I—'

The sound of her uncle calling their names interrupted Leo and together they glanced towards the open bedroom door.

'We're in here,' Leo called back, picking the baby up and handing her over to Gila. With a lingering kiss to Arabella's head, he straightened as Art rushed into the room.

'Oh, it's true. Maggie said Leo called in to collect your bag,' Gila's uncle gushed, moving closer. 'Oh, my goodness, you've really had the baby.'

Gila reached out and caught Leo's fingers. Smiling at him, she searched his face, but found nothing to indicate something was amiss. Perhaps she'd imagined his worried expression and tightness in his movements.

Turning back to her uncle, Gila laughed. 'We did. Come and meet your great-niece.'

Art walked nearer and glanced down at the baby. 'Oh, she's a darling, isn't she? I also wanted to tell you that the road is clear and free from oranges.'

'Finally.' Leo chuckled, removing the stethoscope from his neck and dropping it onto the chair.

Art nodded, his eyes not leaving Arabella. 'She's so small. Are babies always this tiny?'

'She is,' Gila agreed, then reassured him, 'She's early, but she'll soon gain weight. Apart from that, she's fine.'

'Congratulations, both of you,' Art said. 'Your baby is beautiful, but your lives are about to get noisy and busy.'

Gila laughed and glanced at Leo, her heart hitching when she noticed that he wasn't laughing with them, instead his thoughtful gaze was fixed firmly on their sweet baby daughter.

Leo hadn't heard wrong. He'd prayed during the car journey that he had, but the sound he'd picked up when he'd listened to Arabella's heart was just as he thought. When they arrived at the hospital, the doctors soon confirmed his fears. Their daughter had a suspected heart murmur.

Pushing open the door to the room Gila had been allocated, Leo paused on the threshold taking in his wife as she nestled Arabella in her arms. Rooted to the floor by the sheer scene of love before him. A true and pure love. A mother and child's love. Clear in the way Gila held and looked at their daughter, softly whispering comforting words to her.

Love.

That special sentiment that filled a person's life with meaning. A reason for living each and every day. Possessions might look fine and pretty, but they didn't fill a person's heart with light and laughter. They didn't calm a man's soul the way true love did.

The news he'd come here to give Gila would test that connection of love and probably theirs as well. He wasn't too conceited to admit it scared him. He'd already let this woman down. He'd promised Gila a life of happiness, when all he'd managed to do was inflict heartache on her without meaning to. He'd emotionally locked her out when he should have smashed through the difficulty and found a way to say the words crammed inside him.

'Hey,' he greeted, stepping further into the room. He wasn't going to avoid this moment any longer. He suspected Gila already sensed something was off because of the way she'd kept glancing at him during the car ride to the hospital. Plus, he needed to make a phone call after he spoke with her. One that wouldn't wait.

She smiled, her beautiful smile that always hit him hard in the centre of the heart. The one that had captured him the first time she sent it his way. The one he'd fallen in love with.

'Gila, we need to talk.'

Apprehension erased the happiness from her expression and he faltered as he crossed the room. Here was his small perfect family. His purpose for waking each day. The real reason his heart took each single beat. He hated doing it, but she had to know the truth. He refused to keep secrets from her. He'd done it once and look at what happened. It was time to find out her thoughts, before someone else accidentally let slip about the murmur. And she would hate him if that happened.

He reached the bed and sat down. The thin mattress giving underneath him. Swallowing, he took a moment, before he said, 'Gila, the doctors have checked over our sweetheart.'

Gila frowned and waited for him to continue. 'Yes, the midwife who brought her back just now told me they'd finished, but she never said anything else. Is everything okay?'

Leo hesitated, before meeting her gaze. Seeing the concern in her eyes, he stiffened his spine. God, how he loved this woman. How he ached to protect her from any worries, but this was their child and she needed to know.

'Leo?' she quizzed.

His eyes moved to their daughter. The corner of his mouth twitching as he took in her sweet baby face. How could anyone think babies were ugly when they were born? His little girl wasn't. Without thought or effort, love flowed through him with more force than a monsoon. There wasn't anything he wouldn't do or give for his little girl.

'Something's wrong, isn't it?' Gila whispered.

He nodded, not surprised by her question. As a midwife, she'd easily recognise the signs when the medical staff were concerned for a baby's well-being. No doubt she'd already figured out the truth. 'Yes.'

She sighed impatiently. 'I'm not stupid, Leo. I know the protocol, and from what I can tell you're all keeping something from me. Something concerning my child. And I want to know what it is. In fact, I insist you tell me right now.'

He grasped her hand and cradled it in his own. Cupping the warm palm with his cold one. Clearing his throat, he swallowed the dryness in his mouth and said, 'Arabella has a suspected heart murmur.'

She stared at him for a moment, before nodding and shifting her gaze to their daughter. 'Are they sure?'

He gently squeezed her hand. 'Yes.'

'I see. And why wasn't I told?'

Her lack of surprise told Leo his instinct had been correct. She'd guessed something was wrong. Probably worked out what it was during the car journey and before they reached the hospital.

'You knew,' Gila accused, pinning him once again with her gaze. 'At home when you listened to her heart. You knew then, didn't you? And yet you never said a thing. Why not?'

He held up a hand, to stop her from continuing. 'I suspected, but I hoped I was wrong. Cardio is not my speciality. But, yes, I thought I could hear whooshing as I listened to her heart. But I wanted a second opinion first.'

'I don't understand why you didn't tell me,'

she said. 'At least mention your concerns. I'm Arabella's mother. I'm your wife.'

'I didn't want to worry you until I knew there was a definite reason to,' he repeated, desperate to reassure her. To explain there was nothing thoughtless or calculated behind his thinking. He merely thought it best to be sure.

She tutted and pulled her hand away. Averting her face, she tightened her arms around their child, as though to shield and defend her from Leo and the world. 'Keeping things from me again, Leo. Is this how it's always going to be?'

He winced as he took the hit. Yes, it hurt but he deserved it. Of course she'd think the worst, and he couldn't deny it. But this time he'd kept quiet because he'd wanted to be sure of his facts first. To save her from unnecessary worry. She'd just given birth and was so happy. The notion of having to crush her delight and replace it with anxiety, even for a while, when it might be unnecessary had kept him quiet. Nothing else. 'This isn't the same, Gila.'

She glanced back to him, her grey eyes flashing like lightning in a stormy sky. And mingled in the silvery depths was another emotion. One he recognised easily because he'd seen it so many times over the last few months. That unwelcome companion that often seemed to shadow his wife's estimation of him. Disappointment.

'Isn't it?' she asked quietly. Her anger from moments before disappearing as resignation replaced it. The sigh that followed both heavy and tired.

'No. I just wished to make sure first,' he insisted, hoping to make her understand. This really wasn't the same as when Jodie died. He wasn't turning into himself, unknowingly pushing everyone—her—away. He'd just figured waiting until he could give her more information was a wiser decision.

She shook her head. 'Doesn't this sound familiar, though?'

He reached for her hand again, but she shifted it away, tucking it underneath Arabella's bottom. Hiding it from him and making it plain she didn't welcome his touch. 'Don't do this, Gila. We're both emotional and worried right now, but—'

'There's nothing wrong with my daughter,' she insisted, her grey irises daring him to argue. 'I don't care what you or any other doctor in this hospital thinks. My baby is perfect and she will be fine. I'm her mother and I know it's the truth deep down inside. I would sense if something was wrong with her.'

'Gila, please. You may well be right, but—'

'I *am* right!' she vowed, glancing down at Arabella. She fiddled with the pink knitted hat their daughter was wearing. 'I know I am.'

Leo nodded, accepting it was what she believed and refusing to argue with her. He had no reason to until they knew what they were dealing with. 'All right, but we have to do the checks.'

She huffed and twisted further away. Closing herself off from him and what he was saying. Doing to him what he'd not so long ago done to her. Was this immense pain ripping through his heart how he'd made her feel?

'You should go now,' she said quietly. 'I need to sleep.'

'Would you like me to put Arabella in her cot?' Leo asked, nodding towards the hospital cot at the side of the bed.

Gila shook her head and hugged their daughter closer. 'No, I can do it.'

Leo stood, deciding it best to leave her alone while he made his phone call. They would talk when he returned, but first he had to make the call. It was important. 'Okay.'

Walking away, he paused at the door. 'Please don't shut me out, Gila.'

She waited until he'd stepped through it, before replying softly, 'That's your forte, Leo, not mine.'

CHAPTER TWELVE

LEO PUSHED OPEN the glass doors, exiting the baby unit, and finally allowed hope to ease its warmth through his cold, numb body. Since confirmation of his initial diagnosis, he'd switched into his detached and cool professional doctor vibe, instead of giving into the out-of-control parental worry hovering and threatening to wipe away some of the joy of his daughter's unexpected arrival.

Their precious little girl had a congenital heart defect, or, in layman's terms, had been born with a heart problem and while his clinical brain focused on the fact that many babies were born with heart murmurs and lived perfectly normal, healthy lives, his same rational mind refused to forget that there was a rare but slim chance that a defect could turn out to be a major issue for his child.

It all depended on what type of heart murmur Arabella suffered. After leaving Gila in her room, he'd immediately telephoned a friend—a heart specialist—and asked him to examine Arabella. It wasn't that he didn't trust the hospital's doctors, but this man was one of the top cardio experts in the world and his little girl deserved to see the best if Leo could pull the strings and make it possible. He didn't care if it ruffled egos or upset any member of the staff. He was doing this for Gila and Arabella. Doing everything he could to make sure he didn't let another person down. That he didn't let Gila down again.

Fortunately his friend had readily agreed and was right at this moment examining Arabella. Leo had chosen to leave the room and wait outside, not trusting himself not to give into the impulse to snatch his child away from the people who were trying to help.

Suddenly exhausted, Leo lowered onto a nearby chair positioned against the corridor's wall. Closing his eyes, he blocked out the sounds of the busy hospital all around him, his thoughts shifting to his wife and her earlier reaction to the news.

Recalling the stubbornness in Gila's tone and the protective flash in her eyes caused him to smile despite the gloom of his mood. She was right when she insisted their daughter was perfect. Arabella was, no matter what was going on inside her tiny, delicate body. Seeing Gila so defensive and dismissive of any criticism of their baby filled him with strength and wonder. Amazed yet again by the intensity of a mother's love for her child.

Gila would never reject or feel inconvenienced by her child the way his parents often had. She'd fight any battle, big or small, to protect their daughter. Because despite her knowing the medical realities and possible ins and outs of such a condition, the fierce glimmer in her eye showed clearly that she thought he and the doctors in this hospital were all fools. When she looked at Arabella, she saw only a beautiful newborn baby. She would never view her as a problem or an inconvenience.

Opening his eyes, he tilted his head back against the wall. Yes, a mother's love was a powerful thing, and today Gila had displayed its real and full magnificence and he felt privileged and proud to have witnessed it.

She'd also made it clear how unimpressed she was with him and the way he'd kept quiet about his concerns over Arabella's heart. Yet again he'd chosen the wrong course when hoping to safeguard his wife. But he honestly hadn't wanted to scare or worry her until there was cause to.

Instead, though, he'd given her a new motive not to trust him. After everything they'd been through today, bringing Arabella into their lives. The fragile bridge they'd created working together for their child's sake, he'd broken by staying quiet. When she'd asked what was wrong why hadn't he just told her? When he'd heard the whooshing noise, a sign of turbulent blood flow, while listening to Arabella's heart, why hadn't he asked Gila's opinion? Included her in the discovery. Because the old part of him wanted to shoulder all the stress and save her from it. And if he was really honest, he didn't want to accept that there might be a problem with their daughter's health, either. Didn't want to face that stark reality when, as Gila had already stated, to them Arabella was perfect. Or allow the idea that someone he loved might be snatched away again, and him incapable of doing anything to prevent it.

And now he sat here alone waiting for the specialist's verdict because he'd messed up for the hundredth time. Or so it felt. Praying for a positive outcome, while people passed by, concerned only with their own problems and troubles. Knowing that there was nothing he could do to aid his child except beg whatever God cared to listen to his pleas to save his baby from the worst possible scenario as he impatiently waited to hear how poorly his baby girl really was.

How many more times must he stand alone? Always unassisted and solitary. Helpless to change the inevitable. He was tired and fed up with dealing with problems without someone to turn to. Without a shoulder to rest upon. His counsellor during their sessions encouraged him to share his feelings, but Leo didn't really want to talk to the man. It was Gila he yearned to unburden his soul to. Gila he wanted to hold close and confess his inner fears to. She was the one whose opinion he longed to hear. Whose arms he craved to encircle him when his body threaten to buckle. But how could he expect her to be there for him, when he shied away from letting her in? From accepting her strength and wisdom when his own faltered.

The sound of a door opening and heavy footsteps drew his attention from his bleak thoughts. He turned and watched his friend, the specialist, walk briskly towards him, tweed jacket flapping, his expression void of any clue or indication whether the update he brought on Arabella was bad or good.

A shiver prickled over Leo's neck and his mouth dried. His gaze not leaving his friend's face even though his eyes burnt from watching him. Rubbing his clammy hands against his jeans, Leo ignored the increasing dense thud of his rapid heart pounding in his ears.

Reaching Leo, his friend stopped and removed his silver glasses. With a sigh, he took the seat next to him and cleared his throat before meeting Leo's gaze. 'Let's go somewhere private and talk, shall we?'

Gila wasn't sure how she ended up sitting in the hospital garden. After she'd been checked over, the doctor on duty had happily declared she was fine and fit for a woman who'd recently given birth and discharged her. The fact she lived with a doctor no doubt eased any of the man's concerns, but Gila couldn't leave because half an hour ago a midwife had arrived at her room and whisked Arabella off for further checks and tests over at the special baby unit.

Gripping her hands together, she sighed. At least this time she knew why they had taken her and wasn't left frustrated and wondering why the midwives wouldn't give clear answers to her questions.

The fragrance of the plant to the left of the bench filled the air. Gila didn't recognise the shrub, but the fragrance reminded her of the baby lotion she'd bought for Arabella. One she hadn't yet used. Same as all the other items she'd gathered over the last few months for her baby.

Dashing a tear away, she folded her arms and fixed her gaze on the trickling water bubbling from the stone fountain in the centre of the garden. The sound was supposed to be comforting and relaxing, but Gila found it annoying and wished it would stop. How could she feel calm when her mind resembled a mixed pot of disturbed thoughts?

A heart murmur wasn't so worrying. Not always. Babies were often born with them and no one really understood why. Many were nothing to be concerned over and disappeared within days or weeks.

But every time Gila considered it, all she could see was the image of Leo's face when he'd listened to Arabella's heart, followed by his lying. He'd said he'd wanted to save her unnecessary worry. Huh! Just the same way he'd wanted to protect her from his depression after his sister's death. But was it protection or simply lying? She wasn't some innocent who needed hiding from life and its ugliness. She was a trained midwife, who understood how these things happened sometimes. Leo should have respected her rights professionally as a midwife and Arabella's mother, and as a new parent to hear the truth straight away. But no, he'd made a decision and done everything his own sweet way. Was the pattern of Leo shutting her out repeating itself yet again? Had all their talking over the past few days meant nothing? Had his ears been as muffled as they had been in the past? Did he still harbour the misconception that she needed to be screened from the world and its harsh realities? Hadn't she experienced and dealt with more than her share of unpleasant things during her childhood?

She sucked in a breath and made herself view the situation from his perspective. Maybe that last one was partly why he did it. He'd said he wished to wait until he had all the facts before including her, but did he also hope to save her from facing it because she'd been subjected to so much trauma and upset during her early years?

Well, she didn't require gentle handling when it concerned their daughter. The child her empty arms seriously ached to hold but couldn't because her poor little girl was undergoing more tests. Gila had asked which ones, but the midwives on duty, supposedly her friends and colleagues, were decidedly vague and rebuffed her questions with lectures on her need to rest and sleep. They were kind, but she knew when she was being brushed off. She'd done the same to her own patients in the past, usually when they didn't have the medical answers and were shy of causing the parents unnecessary apprehension. Now having experienced how annoying it was to be the parent being fobbed off, she vowed never to do it again. From now on she would be straight with all her mums and dads. It wasn't nice being kept in the dark and treated like a breakable new mother on the verge of shattering. She hated it. No, she *resented* it. How dared they treat her in such a way? They should know better. As Arabella's mother, she had more rights than any other human being in this hospital.

She also wanted to yell and scream because once again she was going through a horrible confusing hell and doing it completely alone. Leo had disappeared and her child was having who knew what done to her and no one, not one single person, thought that she might want to be with her. Or how *she* might be terrified and feeling utterly useless and superfluous while others fussed around her baby.

'So this is where you are.'

A familiar deep voice spoke behind her. One she wasn't particularly keen on hearing right now. Reluctantly, she turned her head and took in her husband, standing with both hands resting on his hips. Tiredness lined his face, and there was something in his gaze she couldn't decipher.

'They've taken Arabella again,' she said, suspecting he knew already. But she didn't know what else to say to him. What did a wife say to the husband who dashed off and left her on her own? Earlier, during Arabella's birth, they had been as one, so together, a proper couple again, but now she could hardly stand to look at him.

'I know. She's in the baby unit waiting for us to collect her.'

Leo strolled over and settled next to Gila on the bench. Without saying a word, he reached over and hauled her into his arms, and whispered, 'I called a friend—a cardiologist—he knows his stuff. One of the best. I asked him if he would come to the hospital to examine Arabella and he did.'

'Is that where you've been?' she asked, scared to hear the rest of what was coming. Hiding from the inevitable was irrational and impossible, but suddenly she desperate wished to delay it. She'd imagined Leo somewhere else, doing other things, *what* she wasn't certain, but she'd never considered he'd be calling in favours from medical associates or friends.

Leo kissed her head and squeezed her tighter. 'Yes.'

So instead of abandoning them as she'd feared, Leo had been making sure their daughter was seen by an expert in the field. 'When you disappeared, I thought… I know I told you to go, but—'

'I'm sorry I left you for so long, but I realised I wasn't your favourite person and I wanted to speak with the man. He's a friend and I knew he was only in London this week, visiting family. Normally he's based in Scotland. When he agreed to come to the hospital straight away, I figured you'd want me to find out his prognosis immediately.'

She nodded and asked, 'What did he say?'

Leo cuddled her tighter. 'He suspects the problem lies with a leaky valve. There are no guarantees, but he's pretty confident that over the next few months Arabella's heart will mend itself. She'll need regular check-ups to monitor her heart through follow-up appointments, but he sees no reason why we can't all go home and let nature do its own healing with no other interference from us.'

Gila smiled and then burst into tears. Their little girl wasn't completely out of danger, but the murmur wasn't so serious it required an operation. With time the heart would mend allowing Arabella to enjoy a full and normal life. They weren't going to lose her. She was going to be all right.

She smiled through her tears. Wiping at her damp face with the cuffs of her jumper, she sniffed. 'Oh, Leo, that's wonderful.'

He chuckled and agreed. 'It is.'

Quietly absorbing the good news, Gila slowly leaned her body into Leo's. She turned her face into his chest, the thick material of his blue-checked shirt rough against her cheek. But she didn't pull away, the feel of it and the firm wall of his body beneath too comforting to leave. For the last few hours she'd refused to listen to the hateful voices whispering inside her head, goading her. Voices whose only aim was to fill her with doubt and questions. But she'd adamantly refused to listen to them. Deep down inside she'd known her darling baby was fine, and now Leo had confirmed that belief. Her mother's intuition spot on when it came to her daughter.

'Leo,' she said, fiddling with one of the buttons on his shirt. 'I have a confession to make.'

Leo shifted and tilted her face upwards. 'You do?'

'I owe you a big apology because I'm guilty of believing the worst of you. I'm ashamed to admit that for the last half-hour I've been thinking the most terrible things about you. Really awful thoughts.'

To her surprise he laughed. 'You have?'

She nodded. 'I asked one of the midwives where you were and she'd said you'd gone. I felt so alone after you left my hospital room and I assumed you'd left Arabella and me because of the way I reacted...'

'You thought I'd deserted you both when you needed me?' he asked, guessing the rest.

She nodded and dropped her head to his shoulder. Not eager to see his displeasure. 'I did.'

Leo sighed and tugged her closer. His strong arms wrapping her in the cocoon of his embrace. 'Sweetheart, it's going to take time learning to trust one another again. But we've the rest of our lives together to do so. I'm not worried, nor should you be. We just need time.'

She glanced up at him and quizzed, 'You're not mad?'

He thought for a moment, then shook his head. 'If you'd disappeared after our conversation about the heart murmur, considering the last few months, and the way I behaved before, I probably would've deduced the same thing. But I swear to you, on this old thing called my heart, that you and our daughter are everything I want in life, and I'm not going anywhere without you both. I promise, I'll never leave you physically or emotionally again. All I'm guilty of is wanting to get the specialist here and I'm afraid I pushed everything and everyone else from my thoughts while I did so.'

Gila sighed. 'I hate being like this…doubting you and—'

Leo put his finger on her lips. 'It's understandable. Just give me the opportunity to dispel those fears. It's all I ask. I love you, Gila. Please give me a second chance to prove how much. You know, the counsellor helped me with accepting that nothing I did would ever have helped my sister, but on those hard dark days when I struggled, it was the thought of you that got me through them. I didn't know if you'd ever forgive me or even if we would have a future together, but just the notion of you being in my life in any small way was what pushed me to fight. You are the splendour in my life. These last few days together have been precious to me. Living together, properly talking to each other. Admitting feelings I've never told another soul. And now we have Arabella. If you decide that all you want is to be friends while we raise our child, then I'll accept that. I'll take whatever you feel able to give.'

Gila stared into the face of the man she still loved, suddenly convinced a life minus him would be nothing but an empty one. One lived but never fully enjoyed. Like the sky without rain, or grass without soil. She'd tried for four months to give up their love and hated every minute. Four long months merely existing through each day. She refused to live the rest of her life in such an empty way. Not when she didn't have to.

'Is that what you want?' she asked. 'To be friends and nothing else?'

Leo shook his head. 'No. I want to come home…to you.'

'You do?' she whispered.

He placed two fingers against her top just where her heart lay beneath. 'In there. I want to go home inside your heart.'

Gila swallowed hard. She'd thought to use their week together to say goodbye to their relationship, confident she already understood the wishes of her own heart. What a stupid arrogant fool she was. No, not a fool, but a coward. Running away, instead of fighting for her marriage. Brooding when Leo's own strength called for bolstering. He'd fallen, and instead of picking him up, she'd walked away and sulked.

Please give me a second chance to prove how much.

And he'd asked for a second chance, when *she* should be asking for the same. No, not asking, but begging. She'd picked the easy choice and left their marriage because she hadn't liked the unfamiliar turn it had taken. Like the insecure child she'd once been, too scared to stand and face a situation she found uncomfortable, she'd packed a suitcase and left. But she wasn't a child any longer. She was a strong woman and Leo had helped her become *that* woman with his love and understanding. He'd encouraged and filled her with confidence, yet when he'd needed her the most, she'd failed in not returning that same self-belief.

So yes, she too needed to plead for a second chance. Not just Leo. Because her insecurities had almost robbed them of something very precious. Their marriage. And now it was time for her to be brave and fight for it. Fight for him.

Licking her lips, she said, 'I have a condition first.'

Leo's gaze searched her face. 'Which is?'

'That you give *me* a chance to prove to *you* how much I love you. I let you down, Leo. So I have as much to prove as you.'

'You didn—' he began, but she stopped him.

Covering his mouth with her finger, she shook her head. 'I did. The truth is, I don't understand how love works. Perhaps you can teach me how to do it properly.'

A faint smile tugged at his lips. 'I can do that. It might take a lifetime, though. Loving someone is a special art and should never be rushed.'

She smiled and laughed. 'I promise to be a good pupil, teacher.'

'I need a promise from you,' Leo said, kissing the pad of her finger, still resting against his lips.

'Yes?' she asked.

'Help me learn how to open up when I need to talk. The counsellor's fine, but he's not *you*. You get me better than anyone. It's *you* whose judgement I respect and desire. The last four months have been hell and lonely. I miss you, Gila. Help me learn how to be a better, more open man. One who deserves your love.'

Ignoring her sudden tears, Gila nodded. She could do as he asked. It might take time and many mistakes, but she promised to love this man the way he desired. The way she desperately wanted to. Their relationship had stalled because they'd both made mistakes and resorted to old familiar habits. Ones learnt before they'd ever met. But the best thing with bad habits was that they could be broken and new patterns learnt.

'There's something I'd like you to do,' she said. Reaching into her coat pocket, she took out a ring. A plain simple circle of gold whose symbolism carried so much.

Leo frowned at the sight of it, and then met her gaze. 'Your wedding ring.'

She nodded and held it up between them. 'I kept it under the pillow during Arabella's birth and brought it with me. Like a lucky talisman, I suppose.'

It didn't make sense considering their recent separation, but right now little made much of any. Her fingers were trembling as she held it out to him. 'Will you please put it back where it belongs?'

His eyes widened as he absorbed her words. 'Are you sure it's what you want?'

She nodded. No doubts or concerns murmured to her, just clear certainty that this was the right decision. Every part of her soul urged her to return home in every sense. To repair the broken pieces of their relationship, not with unstable, flimsy patches of promises, but with firm and strong reinforcements made from sturdy and formidable love.

'If you need more time,' he offered.

She shook her head. 'I don't.'

'If I replace the ring then you can't leave again. Whatever problems come along we deal with them by staying under the same roof,' Leo said.

She smiled. 'I agree. I promise to stay put if you promise to talk to me. We're stronger together, Leo. It's taken me a long time to understand that I am no longer alone and I'm determined to make sure that you never will be, either.'

She lifted his hand and placed it against her chest. 'I'm asking you to come home, Leo.'

Leo took the circle of gold from her, and slowly and carefully slid it back onto her finger. Lifting her hand, he kissed the band where it sat snuggly against her skin. 'I'll never give you another reason to take it off again, I swear. You're right. Together we're whole.'

Gila sighed, content and happy. Glancing at the man she loved so desperately, she said, 'Let's collect our daughter and take her home.'

Leo smiled and kissed her hand again.

'With you and Arabella it's the only place I ever want to be. But first I have to do something.'

'What?' she asked.

'Kiss you,' he said.

And so he did. And together they finally returned home to that place they were always meant to be.

EPILOGUE

GILA KISSED ARABELLA'S dark head and breathed in the mixture of soap, baby lotion and sweet little girl that made up her daughter's unique smell. As she rearranged the long ivory-coloured antique gown her daughter wore, a happy peacefulness slipped through her. A familiar feeling these days and she treasured it.

At six months old, her gorgeous baby girl glowed with health and, so far, it appeared her tiny little heart was doing as the doctors hoped and mending naturally. Yet again the human body's ability to heal amazed Gila and she thanked the heavens for the miracle.

Glancing at the clock on the tall city church tower, she smiled when it struck one o'clock. All around friends, family and colleagues manoeuvred their way inside the church building, all there to witness and celebrate Arabella's christening.

After several days of rain, the sun had chosen to reappear that morning and its warm rays heated the busy city and put everyone in a good mood.

'You okay?'

Gila leaned into the man whose arms encircled them. 'I'm a mixture of excited and nervous. How about you?'

'Nah, our Arabella's got this,' Leo answered. 'She's a scene stealer whatever she does. I can't see today being any different. Not our little star.'

All the troubles, disappointment and fears were behind them. These days they continued to move forward, building their relationship and family. Both having learnt from the mistakes they'd stupidly committed. Each determined to make a life together where they talked to one another, even when it was hard and tough. And sometimes it was, but together they managed and worked through it.

They were a family who'd learnt to share and grow. More so since Arabella's arrival. They'd fought their wobbly beginning and survived. No more hiding or trying to shield the other and especially no leaving. Oh, no, her suitcase stayed under the bed and she planned for it to remain there gathering dust, between holidays.

She grinned and turned slightly in Leo's hold. In his dark suit he made her mouth water. Later, she would definitely be helping him out of it when they returned home. His shirt and tie, too.

'You know I love you, don't you?' she said.

Leo's eyes glimmered with happiness and mischief. 'Behave, Mrs Wright, or I'll ravish your pretty mouth right here in front of everyone.'

'In front of a church?' she teased, arching her eyebrows. 'What a naughty man you are.'

Leo chuckled. 'I'm pretty sure the guy in the sky will understand. You're my soulmate, why wouldn't I want to kiss you?'

Gila smiled and hugged their precious daughter closer. Yes, they'd all be having an early night. When she'd met and fallen in love with Leo, he'd given her more than just a love affair. Right here in his arms he'd given her somewhere to belong, a place that would always be her true home.

'Are my special girls ready?' Leo asked, dropping his arms to offer her his hand.

Gila took it and smiled up at the man she adored. 'Always, Leo. For you, always.'

* * * * *